About Mary

About Mary

lonely boy

Copyright © 2022 lonely boy

Paperback: 978-1-63767-760-5
eBook: 978-1-63767-761-2
Library of Congress Control Number: 2022903501

All rights reserved. No part of this publication may be reproduced, distributed, or transmitted in any form or by any electronic or mechanical means, without the prior written permission of the publisher, except in the case of brief quotations embodied in critical reviews and certain other noncommercial uses permitted by copyright law.

This is a work of fiction.

Ordering Information:

 BookTrail Agency
8838 Sleepy Hollow Rd.
Kansas City, MO 64114

Printed in the United States of America

Dedicated to
The LOVE of *MY* LI*F*E

Mary lay there in her hospice bed wondering what happens, where she goes in a few minutes or hours. Would her sixty three years of struggle to survive bring her to a place of eternal happiness or would her love for one man punish her to everlasting hell.

Jim clasped her hand so tight not wanting her to go. Mary is his life. They were lucky they found each other though society if it knew, might think differently. To this moment it was their secret. Connected by every vibration of every cell of both of their bodies, their souls, their hearts, their minds, so connected that even if miles apart they would still know exactly how the other was feeling. People wonder what true love is, well Mary and Jim were the ultimate real deal.

Some would say 'oh it will be a happy day for her' while every part of Jim's body screams aloud 'please let her stay for another while'. Her breathing weakens a little and Jim slightly chokes in sympathy and strengthens their grip. Then a little silence as he wonders is she on the way out, but no Mary's eyes open with such a youthful sparkle and look into Jim's like the very first time that happened about twenty years ago on that miserable damp day on the sideline of a mucky soccer pitch while watching their respective little darlings play. The day their eyes met, their love began. There was no turning back.

Right now the thoughts of death disappear, their eyes smile with love into each others as they relive their times together. These few minutes or hours are the most precious. Let them last forever. Presense needs no time, true love needs no words.

Twenty years earlier... "Go" Mary roared with all her lungs and more as her son passed through the backs with only the goalie between him and what seemed like olympic gold for this near twelve year old. With such enthusiasm Junior drew a kick and the ball sailed wide of the post. "Well for fuck sake" Mary cried as if the world fell apart, she crouched down, turned around and looked up to see the kindest eyes of this total stranger smiling into hers, knowing exactly what she was feeling. With the sudden realisation that it was only the first half, of the first round of the local parishes league they both burst out laughing. Their eyes remained fixated, Mary put her hand out slightly as did Jim but they both realised that it wasn't the thing to do. From that very moment to this nobody ever knew. Mary soon turned to watch her Junior run all over the pitch while Jim's son Graham shivered on the other wing with very little interest in getting involved.

What happens in your upper body when you know you have met someone really special, your breathing gets shallow and faster, maybe your heartbeat increases. Neither Jim nor Mary were remotely ready or available and yet something had happened, and both felt it.

Jim was married to Joanne, a successful solicitor in a large firm in the city. She was a few years older, studied hard, worked hard, and brought work home, spoke about nothing else other than their son Graham, a quiet boy, a bit of a loner who spent most of his time in his bedroom. Jim on the other hand was a lovely normal affable guy who worked as a store manager in a local supermarket. That's where they met. Being single Jim often worked the evening shift when Joanne would be darting in for her deli delights. They would often have a little chat, Jim doing his job and Joanne reading too much into it. Weeks and months rolled on and Joanne plucked up courage to invite Jim to a colleagues wedding down the country. A couple of drink dates preceded the wedding date. A bit of fun, Joanne on her best behaviour trying to be less posh and more like Jim though she did warn him a couple of times that there would be a few barristers there and maybe a judge or two, all taking place in a very old country house hotel. Jim was unphased thinking sher there will be a bar and surely a few sound lads around. Yes there was a bar but the clientele all in formal wear lacked any vestige of normality, and if they were there they were all putting on a good front. What is it about lawyers they think the world revolves around them, the power of constantly putting people down must go to their heads. The speeches were all about this case and that, foreign holiday pranks which were about as stale as old bread, false laughter, the few yachting stories repeated for the umteenth time, all for a couple who were obviously introduced to each other by their mothers! Lucky for Jim he came from a large family of musicians and dancers so he was able to swing and jive Joanne around the dance floor for the night, with the odd pint thrown in while she did her duty as lawyers do. It was more like a networking event for junior barristers than a wedding. There were several of those awkward introductions 'Jeremy this is my friend Jim. So what do you do Jim....I work in Treacy's supermarket... Oh' end of conversation. Luckily Jim couldn't really care. Being a people person he comes across all types from the pompous to the paupers, the latter he considers much more interesting. The posh and pompous seem to work together, dine together, holiday together and are most socially inept with anybody outside their little bubble. Maybe the country solicitors were different but certainly this lot from the city were dangerously full of their own importance.

All of a sudden at quite an early hour the crowd dwindled, well disappeared, so our brave couple and a few loud legal louts headed for the residents bar, which was more like a plush sitting room with a lovely open fire and a few red deer staring down on them. A grand place for a few brandies. She was well able to throw down a few. The more relaxed Joanne was making a rare appearance. Her boss was gone and here she was with quite a hunk, and a room booked on the left wing. She cozied up to Jim and bagan asking the usual questions...did you enjoy the day, the meal, the dancing, and she apologised for having to go off talking to colleagues and introducing him to the dick Jeremy. Her words were getting a bit more choice and Jim realised that she wasn't quite as posh as she was letting on to be. She was slurring a little at this stage as she asked Jim about his previous love life and giving some details of her own which seemed rather limited.

Shall we go upstairs she muttered and added she hoped he didn't mind but the only room she could get was a double. Jim thought, not that he had much choice in the matter, but if they didn't go now he'd be carrying her up, though he would have killed for one more drink.

He threw off his fancy clothes and jumped into bed. Some time later Joanne reappeared from the bathroom, what took her so long god only knows. She wore a beautiful long fawn silky nightdress, hair combed out, serious make-up removed but still covered in something. It was like she had completely sobered up and re-entered with a sense of purpose, with something in one hand. Jim being the forever gentleman pulled back the quilt. His mate seemed a little nervous, sat on the edge of the bed for a minute, it seemed in mental preparation and then slid in and covered over. She looked into Jim's eyes, she had deemed herself ready. With military precision she leaned over and kissed him on the lips. Ok thought Jim, what has she got in mind, but sher we'll go along with it whatever it is. She was wearing one sexy nightdress, that alone would wake up any sleepy male! She obviously meant business he thought as she rubbed her hand up under the t-shirt he was wearing, slowly up and around his chest. She was definitely making all the moves but Jim felt himself getting seriously hard. Its all about the timing. Nobody wants to dissapoint the other especially the first time. She was the type who would get very upset if she didn't come having organised it all. Her many fantasies in the vegetable aisle were about to be out of this world, or dashed. It has literally been years since she had sex with anyone and that was a disaster, a little fellow who just went for the jugular at his pace. Her plans with Jim were for so much more.

"Jim" she said "will you put this on please", oh the fecking things, anyway it was a good way for Jim to slow down a bit, so he took it, put the edge of the packet between his teeth and took out the slippery rubbery condom. It wouldn't roll down his cock, feck it was the wrong way around, eventually he got it right while at this stage she had the t-shirt around his neck and she was kissing him all over his upper body, one hand going down to feel that it was on properly. Doing so set her off completely, oh yes she gasped as she lay her rather flat breasts on his as she moved up and down, her leg flinging over on top. Jim made a move while kissing her and pulled up her nightdress slowly and first placed his whole palm of his hand over her pussy and just rubbed it gently. There was no stopping Joanne as she whipped off Jim's t-shirt and her own nightdress, she wasn't hanging around and was definitely going to be the one in control, on top. As she straddled him Jim thought a bit of foreplay was important as he fingered her clitoris. This drove Joanne mad altogether. She sat up, caught Jim's cock and quickly placed it in her vagina with a satisfying groan, in and in as she moved up and down a little giving it every chance. And then like a jumping jack-ass she banged and banged, so typical of a girl completely unused to the job and not understanding anything about a dual experience, just looking for the jack-hammer action. Oh she roared and shouted and groaned and banged, so much so Jim was expecting a bang on the wall from the guests next-door! She banged so hard at one stage Jim slipped out. She had him back in in seconds and she banged away again. Ah sher Jim was enjoying it but this was a far cry from love, or lust, it was just pure lashing. After a while she came to some kind of climax, Jim wasn't sure whether she had come or had she just ran out of steam. He had anyway and as it wasn't a particularly romantic experience he was able to stay hard. She stalled there for a while eyes closed to feel the experience she had longed for all these years, and after a while she opened her eyes and gently got off and around on her back. Then that awkward bit when Jim realised his condom was not on, it wasn't in the bed so it was obviously still inside Joanne. She quickly put her fingers in and pulled it out and ran to flush it down the toilet. Oh the unromantic necessities of safe sex. She returned and quickly put her nightdress on again and cuddled into Jim. Now this was so much nicer, now they could connect and hug and feel free touching every part of each other's bodies. Jim could kiss Joanne's neck, roll on top, put his hand back up under her nightdress and rub her little breasts, oh so much nicer. He slowly moved his body up and down hers much more organically now, kissing her all over, his cock hardened up again and in a romantic moment was able to slide inside her. Gone were the worries of unsafe sex this was beautiful as he penetrated inside her more and more, and up that other bit, oh my god this was so much better, now she groaned with ease and contentment, loving every move as they both felt every twitch she made, this was pure sexual heaven. Now Jim was full on and to even his surprise along came another ejaculation right inside her beautiful body. She felt it and whispered to him that was the most beautiful feeling, and thanked him. Oh no don't ever thank the man! That's like he was just providing a service. A servant. No no no! Anyway Jim didn't mind though he did grin to himself. He was well done at this stage and kind of proud that he had managed to come twice in such a short time, and being the perfect gentleman was happy that she had a good time and he satisfied her. He wouldn't have minded rolling over on his side of the bed though but Joanne in seventh heaven was well cozied up into him with her arm over his chest. She wanted the night to last forever. Jim knew he couldn't really sleep like that and would be waking up with every little move, but sher he knew he could rest the following day as he wasn't working til Monday.

Morning came and there was no waking Joanne. He lay there for what seemed like hours, thinking. Of the girls he's been with Joanne was definitely the most active by a long shot. God its off-putting, you just wouldn't even look forward to constant gymnastics like that in bed long term, not a bit sensual or loving or satisfying. It seems to be the norm for the older type almost virgins who don't get it very often. Young ones are into the quick blow jobs to quickly satisfy the young studs but for a long term relationship or even marriage Jim wondered could such an active loveless sex life like that be maintained, or would she settle? Would he like to be stuck with Joanne long term, no not really. She's ok but the whole 'keeping up with the Jones' lawyer thing would be truly painful.

Finally there was movement, a bit of a grunt and eyes opening in quick shock at first, then a naughty smile. She made a lame effort to kiss him but it didn't really go anywhere on either side. "Right" she said "I'm going for a shower, unless you want to go first?" A brave, or rather stupid, man might have said he would. She washed and dressed and put on her make-up as if she was going into court in her tight little suit. Why couldn't she be a bit more relaxed in mind and body and be some bit casual? Predictable Jim at least was in jeans and a smart semi-cazh shirt. They packed up fairly quickly with not much said in the bedroom or over breakfast, the stilted conversation, followed by an hour and a half in her beamer on a filthy rotten rainy day, back to Jim's bedsit. There was a little polite kiss and a thank you. He went inside relieved to be alone again in his simple surroundings. Joanne drove off to her little perfect palace, which was partly funded by her hard work and mortgage but mostly by Mummy and Daddy. She did feel slightly different as if she still imagined Jim inside her. She dropped her bag and went upstairs to her bedroom and with these strange feelings she stripped naked and stood in front of the mirror staring at herself. She lowered her fingers to her vulva and into her vagina closed her eyes and fingered herself as if it was Jim coming inside her. She moved to her bed and continued wishing he was there with her and after a while she dozed off into another world. Ya, Jim thought she was a bit of alrigh', the apres sex was good, they had fun, maybe they could get on ok, it might lead to more. She'd certainly be a good catch!

What follows during the next weeks is deep and dark with periods of delight, sorrow, lonliness and questions that delve into your deepest consciousness. Many have been here deciding between life and death but sadly the main concern is 'what would everyone think?'. Yes you guessed Joanne started to feel very queasy and eventually did the test on her own in her bathroom at home, she was pregnant. She had felt it intuitively even before she got queasy and her normal period date came and went. Jim and herself were getting on grand texting each other every couple of nights only to the level of discussing the lovely time they had together which overshadowed and almost eliminated any memories of the wedding itself. Time was not on Joanne's side now. She was on the brink of being offered a partnership in the legal firm in which she diligently worked. They did not want to lose her.

As she stood there in the bathroom she just stared and stared at the positive pregnancy test result facing her next to the hand basin. It was as plain as day and sher she knew it herself. Every emotion under the sun was heaped upon her all at once. Her female hormones and her whole being was warmed by the thought of a baby within her. She vividly feels Jim coming inside her and thinks of it over and over again. For her it was the most beautiful experience, it took her from her never ending organised existance to pure and utter elation. She placed her right hand on her tummy and thought wow there's the beginning of a little human being in there. Then the tears started to roll and wouldn't stop, she felt so alone. She thought of her Mum, but particularly her Dad, oh she cried, she had let him down, what on earth would he think? She was the apple of his eye, he adored her. Would this break his heart? He was quite elderly, this could finish him. Her parents ran an old menswear shop in the midlands, which was in the family for three generations. He hung on for years partly because he just couldn't stop and partly hoping that Joanne's future husband and family might one day take it on. A good old Catholic family, oh god what would they think? She only had one younger brother who was Down syndrome. They had married late in life. Her mother was a right snob but got on grand with her adorable father. Joanne loved her father to bits, how could she ever break this news to him? Would he get a heart attack on the spot? Would he disown her? She couldn't bear to see him cry, or cause any anxiety or shame on him. All her thoughts were for her father, she and her mother didn't really hit it off. Her mother was happy as long as Joanne was doing something she could constantly boast about, but her father was one of those pure old country gentlemen.

    She straightened herself stiffly and thought forget about this little thing and consider getting rid of it fast. Just take a couple of days holiday and go to a clinic. Nobody would know. She gathered herself and headed for her computer downstairs, logged on and typed in 'abortion clinics'. Lots of happy smiley faces with helpful advice. She maintained her stern facade to rationally consider the consequences, it was certainly an option, she needn't even tell Jim. She was sure her friend Jennifer would travel with her as she had done for her a couple of years before. Where was Jennifer now, single, having a fun time, at all the parties, mid thirties, but apparently has her very low days, obviously her abortion is never discussed. Joanne wonders whether Jennifer ever thinks of 'what if' she had the child, would it be a boy or a girl, what would it look like, what age would it be now? They told her at the abortion clinic that it was so small she probably would have lost it anyway. That's what they say to so many girls, you'd think they'd realise word gets around. Ok so there's one, there's the email address, and she types out her email explaining her early stage pregnancy, asked when could she book in and for any advice, but she just couldn't press the send button, several attempts as her heart began to melt and the tears began to flow again, she saved it in draft. This was the most alone time she ever felt in all her life. She flopped into the armchair and sat there in silence for a while and then broke into uncontrollable roaring crying. The poor girl stuck in a time constrained dilemma, she had got caught up in the heat of the moment, and now she is pregnant. Oh why her she thought, didn't this only happen to the loose girls? There she was with her career ahead of her in a really good law firm, and here she is roaring crying, pregnant, alone in her sitting room. She suddenly thought only half this baby is hers, Jim should know, he has a right to know, oh god how to tell him and what will his reaction be? Ah he'll probably say to get rid of it, it's easier that way. Ok Joanne think logically she said to herself. Yes Jim should know, she can't tell him over the phone, she better invite him over. If she's going for termination she would want to do it fast, maybe Jim would go with her, then nobody would know. Jennifer might say something. There was no time to waste so she reached over for the phone and rang him, asking him to come over later, suggesting a pasta supper with a nice Italian red, so as not to let him think anything was up. Thankfully he was off that friday evening as she thought she couldn't put it off for another twenty four hours.

Jim sauntered in around seven o'clock, wine in one hand, a six pack of Fosters in the other. All smiles without a care in the world. There was a nice smell of food in the lovely warm house. He was nice and hungry. Joanne made herself busy around the kitchen and scuttled around moving pots and pans, laying the table, filling a couple of glasses of wine, mixing and serving the spaghetti bolognese. The scene was set for the changing of their lives, one way or the other. Jim was beginning to think there was something up, the atmosphere was that little bit strange, no radio or television noising, he felt a chat coming on, though he wasn't expecting what he was about to hear.

He tore into his pasta making all the right noises, and wondered why Joanne hadn't really touched hers. "Jim, I've something to tell you, I think you have a right to know… (slight pause) … I'm pregnant". "Oh holy suffering mother of Jesus Christ" Jim says, probably not the most appropriate at that particular moment in time "what are you going to do?" oops 'you' was the wrong word. "Well" said Joanne "I was hoping it was 'we', that's why I invited you over. I didn't feel I had the right to terminate myself. We are kind of in this mess together" to which Jim gathered himself and said "of course, don't worry, we'll get through this". Then he added "Terminate, did you say terminate?" his mind understandably a little all over the place. "Ya" she said "I presumed you'd want to get rid of 'this problem' pretty sharp."

What followed was probably the nicest kindest closest few hours Jim and Joanne would ever have together. They discussed everything, I mean everything! They both knew they really only had days to think about it. It was discussions and decisions made under time pressures and stress, but they were both adults and thought they could make sensible rational decisions. They abandoned the kitchen and cozied up in the sitting room in front of the gas log fire. Joanne explained her relationship with her father, how they adored each other, he was an upstanding respected Catholic pillar of the community and parish at home. In fairness to Jim he was only brilliant. He helped her tease out what her father would think in the most understanding detail. If her father knew what would he want, a termination or a grandchild, an heir, possibly the only chance he might ever get. Imagine once they get over everything the delight in the grandfather's face as his grandson or granddaughter would come to visit. His own flesh and blood. Maybe he's more understanding and resilient than he's given credit for, and sher didn't his niece get pregnant and they got over it. Her mother, oh jaysus her mother, Joanne didn't feel any responsibility initially to her reaction. It was all societal issues they seem to be discussing. What would their friends think, her family, would they all disown them? Jim in fairness to him again, as he was quickly working through his six-pack, suggested that all the neighbours and friends, knowing her quite well, might have a right giggle and gossip at her expense, but their likes were all decent enough behind it all and they'd be delighted for them with a gorgeous little grandchild. Oh god Joanne suddenly thought what if her baby was Down syndrome like her little brother Jamie! Oh no she thought she could never ever cope with that. She loved Jamie but I guess since he appeared it was all Jamie with her mother and he almost became her trophy child, he was 24/7. This obviously affected Joanne's relationship with her mother, there simply wasn't time, and any time the mother had needed to be having a break away from the family, usually at the golf club. This instilled a lifelong hatred of golf for Joanne. All of this though probably strengthened her relationship with her father.

What if back in the day they knew the foetus was Down syndrome and they had aborted Jamie? Joanne was often left with Jamie on Saturdays in her teens as her father was in the shop and her mother at the club. Joanne and Jamie had a very special bond and though he was non-verbal they knew exactly what each other was thinking, you'd know by their smiles. Jamie largely made Joanne part of the woman she is today, a decent very hard working dedicated member of society. Alright yes she does have a bit of her mother in her, well engrained, pushing her up the ladder in her legal career. Its all part of it. Without Jamie though she may have grown up to be a right ol' spoilt brat with her quite elderly parents.

The hours rolled on beautifully, the six-pack was well gone though luckily Joanne had some more in stock, Heineken but it didn't matter to Jim. She sipped her wine but took it easy, she wanted her wits about her. She heated up the spaghetti bolognese and they dug into two more lovely bowlfulls on the couch. For both of them, despite everything, they were having a really nice time.

"Ok, enough about my family Jim, what about yours" Joanne said as really she only knew him as a smiley pleasant very helpful guy in the vegetable aisle. Everyone knows a Jim! He was north inner city from a very disjointed family. Jim was one of the lucky ones. His teacher, who was really as much of a social worker as a teacher, a really good person, recommended Jim to his friend who owned a local grocery shop. Even though he didn't finish out his schooling it was a great move for him. He later progressed to a good job in the supermarket when the small shop owner closed up, and he's been there since. One of his brothers, Mick, got a similar opportunity with a local hardware shop. The other three, the two brothers went to England and he hasn't seen them since and his sister god bless her got caught up in drugs with an awful gang and she passed away in her early twenties. His father was a bit strange but always seemed to make out, was always dressed well, wherever he got the money nobody knows and he was always going over and back to England on the boat, wheeling and dealing, and always involved in some new exciting scheme. Jim's poor mother hit the bottle, and you could hardly blame her after more or less bringing up the family as best she could in a fifth storey Corporation flat. She was still alive, barely, in and out of treatment and stays mostly with her spinster sister. She calls into the shop now and again to Jim for a few quid which he always gives her. She doesn't stay long not because she can't be seen talking to him but she can't wait to go and buy a bottle. In Jim's eyes she was a lost cause at this stage.

It was such a completely different upbringing to Joanne's and yet here they are happy out on the couch together getting closer and closer. She wonders silently what they would be like together. Jim is more kind of settling in, looking around the room in the broader meaning of all of that and sher she's 'a bit of all right' as the lads would say, despite her notions and her flat chest, he smiles to himself. He is a man after all, but one with a kind heart.

As the night rolls on Joanne explains to Jim how she never felt so alone after she found out she was pregnant, and asked him not to leave her tonight, she couldn't bear it. They discussed with love and laughter what it would be like to have a little bambino, no sleep, exhausted all the time, a whole change of life, Sunday trips down to the old folks with all the gear, or at least that's what all their friends with babies complain about. They rarely see them anymore, which proves that point!

Every now and again Joanne gets a bit teary mostly when thinking about her father and bringing her family into disrepute, but sher she's in the city, miles away, nobody need know she thinks. There's something about Jamie that really puts her off the idea of an abortion. She loves Jamie beyond words could express and wonders how he would put up with the little one, maybe like a younger brother or sister, or son or daughter that he would never have. How could she possibly deprive him of that, and thinking logically, as Joanne does, maybe Jamie will be living with her at some stage or at least at weekends, holidays or respite for her parents if her father ever gives up the shop. Joanne swings from tears to joy, to tears to practicalities. Jim sips away and in fairness is very comforting to her.

They call it a night and wander away upstairs hand in hand beautifully together. Jim slips in under the sheets and blankets while Joanne has the misfortune of seeing the test kit in the bathroom which sets her off again. Wiping away her wet cheeks she slowly gets into bed and gives Jim a hug. He responds with a bit more physicality thinking that he can't do any more damage at this stage but she declines his advancements and just wants to be close. She didn't want to spoil what was a very special night, and understandably enough she was feeling a bit strange and raw for any kind of sex right now. They both lay there, eyes wide open for quite a while, both considering the unsaid words of what this would be like long term.

Saturday morning and a change for the books. Jim woke up and no Joanne beside him. She had woken at six and at this stage was up and dressed, kitchen all cleaned up and a smell of a good ol' fry-up wafting up the stairs. Jim put on what clothes he had and went down into the kitchen, a hug, a kiss and heard the explanation as expected for the early rise. The happy couple devoured the breakfast while enjoying a good coffee.

Jim had lots worked out in his head and without hesitation one of the most beautiful and romantic moments of their lives was about to take place. He went up behind her at the sink and when she turned around Jim was down on one knee and said "Joanne, will you marry me?" Without hesitation, as she had also worked out that this would by far be the best course of action in this situation, he is a fine man, kind, comforting, hard working, would make a great dad she said "Yes, yes, yes Jim, I will, thank you." How many thoughts can go through a woman's mind in one moment!

From tears and loneliness one morning to such joy twenty four hours later. There was no question at this stage of losing the baby, Joanne had it all worked out, a small wedding, stay in the city until the baby is nearly a year old and sher nobody will know. The anonymity of a city does have serious societal advantages. This almost couldn't happen down the country at that time. She may have had to slip away with a friend. Not too long before that, if maybe from a lower societal strata she would have been sent off to a Magdalene Laundry for a year or two with her baby being sent off for adoption, sold to the U.S. in other words! Society caused and covered up such grief. At least Joanne and Jim could make a life together for themselves and their little one. Your guess is as good as theirs as to how it will all work out. A kept man, with a handy job, with flexible hours, sorted!

Oh what a lovely Saturday! A spin into town, looking around jewellery shops, going back to her favourite one to buy that beautiful ring, down to the pier to put it on and a late lunch in a lovely restaurant overlooking the water. Jim was able to have a couple of pints as Joanne was driving, but she chanced a glass of champagne to celebrate! They stopped off at Jim's place on the way back for him to pick up his gear, he was moving in! Then all that was left was to call her parents with the great news, though unexpected, with no details added. Joanne and Jim made a pact not to tell anyone their private business, not a soul! They were getting married on a Friday, three months later, a small wedding in a secluded location.

Its hard to fool inner city boys though and they certainly don't hold back with their comments. At Jim's stag party down in the local boozer the banter began … "Ah jaysus Jim a 'Monday wedding' on a Friday, go on you good thing." "Up the duff." "Jayz you're no fool, a lawyer, be jaysus ah you're a sly one," "A layin' hen." "Will you g'way outta dat she's not a solicitor is she, jayz that'll come in handy, we'll get special rates." "two for the price of wan, sher you're good on the offers Jim," "G'wan ya boyo." "Get him another pint there he deserves it, and a steak with it, he's a busy man, if ya know whar I mean." "I think you've lost a bit of weight there Jim, all the action, fuck it fair dues to you lad, a fucking solicitor, and I suppose a big ball o'money behind her, jayz fair fucks to you." It was a good ol' night, plenty drink, plenty banter. One of the lads caught Jim in a quiet corner "Jayz Jim are you ok, you're happy enough with everything, are you? Tis a bit of a rush job, I can guess why. Don't do it if you're not a hundred per cent." "Ah sher Anto its ok" Jim says "she's a fine girl, her heart is in the right place. Its all a bit crazy alright, a few months ago there was I minding my own business and now all of a sudden I'm hitched up with a fairly fancy wan and living in a decent detached house, She's alright, you know, she wouldn't exactly be very comfortable in here, and to be quite honest I stick out like a sore thumb in her circles but sher when we're together we're grand, you know. With the little bambino on the way, oh fuck it I wasn't meant to say anything about that, Anto, don't tell anyone will ya, please?" "Ah jayz I won't say a word, sher you know me" Anto replied, and Jim continued "Anto I'm really sorry you're not coming with the lads to the wedding, I'm really sorry, but its only a small family one down the country, you know yourself."

Inner city people are probably the most decent people in the world but boy are they direct. Deep down though, from generations of struggle to survive, they look after each other like a mother looks after her young. "Ah jayz Jim" says Anto " don't worry pal I know the craic, I understand, you know, but I'm going to say one thing to you to you mate, are you listenin', are ya, d'ya hear me, I'm serious, are ya? I mean it. It won't be easy at times, sher fuck it we all know that. There'll be times you'll say what the fuck did I marry her for, was I bleedin' mad, and there'll be the good times which make up for it but Jim promise me this, no matter what you'll come to me and the lads if yous need anything. We're always here for you lad, you know." And god knows he meant it. That's inner city, thick as thieves, salt of the earth.

The hen party was a very different affair, the girls went out for a meal in a nice restaurant on the southside. Two solicitor friends from College and a friend from boarding school, poor girl never met the others before and was sitting at the end away from Joanne. They had gone to a midland boarding school, one full of daughters of strong farmers and business people, about twenty miles from Joanne's home. She was always the last to be collected on Friday evenings after her father shut the shop. Her mother only ever collected her once when there was an important Chamber of Commerce meeting. Joanne used to sit there for hours as all the others were collected before 'milking time' by their fathers in dirty old jeeps or by their mothers in spanking new BMWs. They had an early night, no mention much of Jim and certainly no mention of the 'bun in the oven'. No way was Joanne going to spill the beans. The two solicitor friends did mention when they went to the ladies that Joanne was looking a little pale and drawn. Hmmm yep they wondered why it was all a bit rushed and had never heard of this Jim fellow, they hadn't been at that wedding. They were both in family firms.

The wedding day was similar, a bit of a non event, Joanne's mother not one bit happy with her marrying someone much lower than her, though if the truth be told her mother wasn't exactly royalty! The macra would break out now and again with a good loud hearty laugh. Joanne's father Gerry gave a nice welcoming speech with a nice bit of wit, thanking Joanne for having a nice little inexpensive wedding. Jim's brother Mick was his only guest and best man. He nervously read out a relatively short speech welcoming Joanne into the family, without saying that actually none of the rest of the family even knew Jim was getting married.

Mick doesn't drink so he headed away and the others stayed in the hotel. Everyone was in bed by midnight, everybody quite sober. Joanne was happy there were no incidences and everything had gone off smoothly. Nobody had spotted the bump in her carefully selected more puffy style wedding dress with an over cardigeny thing. Lucky it was winter and she kept it on the whole time.

The relief soon changed to reality. Though they had spent the last three months living together this now was it. That was her big day. She was happy enough though. She hadn't been swept off her feet by a Leonard Cowen lookalike but she had a very decent man in the bed beside her. It was a little awkward as both knew the tradition of a bit of, you know, 'hows your father' on the wedding night. Joanne didn't feel like it but Jim was anxious to mark the occasion. It was all very clinical. With Joanne there was no sucking and biting her nipples, no romantic stubble around her neck, no nipping of ears, no sliding down her body kissing and tongueing her vulva, she hated that, she called it 'animal-like'. But hey we are animals! It was more like "Jim don't put any pressure on my tummy please, stay up" his hands firmly down either side of her, a bit of rubbing of the genitals but that was it. She hadn't come since the previous wedding night. Jim knew the score and knew well what lay ahead of him. She was what the lads used to call 'a frigid', thin, small breasts, never rubbed much, you know the type. Jim though had his own way of making the best of the occasion. On the tills in Treacy's was a fucking beautiful girl called Maag, plump, broad, thick legs, not very tall, generally wearing sexy kind of clothing, black tights and a short black tight skirt. Her breasts were to die for, you could just lose yourself amongst them. She had the sweetest smile and the dimples in that lovely big fat face of hers so pretty. Jim always liked to have the light off so when he was banging away with Joanne he would always think that she was Maag. He imagined her lovely fat body, her huge breasts, he would make lip movements thinking he was going from one nipple to the other and just rubbing his stubble all over her beautiful front. This was heaven. He imagined pulling up her short black skirt up around her middle and pulling her designer silky nickers down to her ankles and with his toes slipping them off one foot, he'd rub his cock up and down a bit on her vulva, slip off to the side and finger her clitoris, which made her groan with delight, a girl who didn't need much foreplay to climax, he imagined getting back on and rising up along her body through her big breasts and his cock finally reaching her big lips. Her tongue would tip the top of his cock and then slowly gradually put her lips on it and suck and suck and then her whole mouth would be around it. Not wanting to miss the real thing he would imagine withdrawing and slipping fairly lively down again, and now hardened to the last the top of his cock would beautifully find its way and steadily feel it sliding in, though she was heavy she was so lovely and tight, and he went right in to that extra inside chamber whatever it is but was in and he pushed and he pressed ever so slightly out and then in harder and deeper and in and in and oh god in unison himself and Maag were completely together and in and in and oh jesus oh god oh jesus it was coming and oh my god here it was with that tingling, shaking, shuddering definite drive of no return up into her goes all his manhood, the greatest feeling in the world, pure heaven, its done its in and their world goes still. And then he wonders has she come as he had got totally carried away. He had heard her roaring in satisfaction. Was he to pretend to give another few jabs just in case, no he thinks she definitely came, confirmed with her saying 'oh god Jim that was fucking amazing'. Wow. But of course it was all in his head. Thankfully the experience is real as he slips his way out of Joanne who lies there as if she was doing her job. Its a sign of what's to come, its hardly going to improve. As long as Jim has his imagination and the shower he'll be grand. What about Joanne, is this what she likes, is she asexual, or would another man, or woman, turn her on? Maybe she's just a once a fortnight, birthdays and Christmas sort of girl, to keep Jim onside. Maybe she thinks that will keep him satisfied. Not the best start on their wedding night!

They get back into their work routine straight away, planning to go on honeymoon at a later date. It keeps everything very low key. Its almost like the wedding never happened, but no it was a reasonably pleasant day. The spring rolls on, and early summer, Joanne disguised everything with flowing summer dresses. Jim just worked away and now did all the shopping according to Joanne's meticulous lists. He mowed the lawn, put out the rubbish, filled the dishwasher and generally became her little slaveboy/handyman, oh and he did most of the cooking, except when he was on a late shift at work. Joanne is a workaholic and didn't know when to turn off. She brought loads of files home and often didn't finish 'til nearly midnight. Life was fairly fucking monotonous really. The baby was due in early August so Joanne took the second half of July, August and some of September off, which fitted in nicely with the courts calendar.

The bouncing little bambino boy came on queue in early August. At eight pounds four ounces how could they explain he was premature, so they took a pound off when telling anyone. Wahoo they got away with it!

Little Graham was a grand little lad. Apart from Jim spilling the beans to Anto at the stag all was ok. The bulk of the childminding duties were left to Jim except for weekends when herself took over. Joanne suggested to Jim that he changed his rota to weekends and evenings which he duly did, that and the creche and it all worked out alright.

This literally, no word of a lie, went on for twelve years! Jim just changed his rota for young Graham's soccer matches. The doting grandparents, now retired, visited now and again, mostly when Jim was working. Anytime Joanne went to a 'legal do' Jim sometimes got a babysitter and went for a pint or two, and also sometimes on a Saturday night after work. Ah life wasn't too bad, sher that's it isn't it.

That is of course until one day, totally unexpectedly, on a miserable Saturday afternoon at an under twelves soccer game when this ray of light lifted her head in disbelief after her son had missed a sitter in front of the goal. Her eyes met Jim's and a dart of energy like lightening shot between them. Oh my good god what was this? Neither were expecting anything. Her smile was infectious, his so kind. Was this literally love at first sight? Or was Jim so fucking bored with his life was he excited to connect with any pleasant young lady? But he knew immediately this was different, he felt a tingling in his body, a shortness of breath, almost a slight anxiety attack. What is it about this woman?

Enough about Jim, this is Mary, who has lived a much more colourful life! This feisty young bright woman has struggled more than most but she rises effortlessly every time determined to have a wonderful life. Everybody just loves her. She has had to be mother and father to her three children. Her husband Marty worked in the brewery. As tradition had it he and his workmates got a pint of the black stuff free every day. Some would go home after it but it only gave a taste of more for Marty and another few lost souls who all couldn't pass the pub on the way back. Most of the others were single though. What a nice guy he was up through his teens, a great footballer which helped him get his good job in the brewery. For a north inner city girl getting hitched up with a brewery boy meant never being short, not having to work outside the home and having lots of time to raise their kids.

For the first few years of married life Marty cashed his weekly pay cheque in the local shop and brought home a few treats, kept the price of a few pints and gave the rest to Mary. Gradually more and more on pints, he was now cashing it in the pub and bringing nothing home. 'How could he' everyone thought, such a fine fella and the most gorgeous young wife and three kids. He went to get dried out a couple of times but it wouldn't last a week. Miraculously he held his job down, its the only thing that gave him some structure in life, but he was a lost cause, a demon for the drink. With some stroke of luck they managed to be in a flat belonging to the brewery and the rent which was reasonable was subtracted weekly before he got his wages. They were nice enough flats. Mary had to rear the family with the childrens allowance money she got and her cleaning jobs, but the worst of it was the abuse. The lovely Marty turned into a right bully after drink, it was more mental than physical but it was every night. Mary would have all the kids in bed by the time he'd come back roaring and shouting. The best nights were when he'd just throw himself on the bed fully clothed and fall asleep. The worst nights were when he'd blame Mary for everything, not putting in enough effort as he'd been working for years, not being a good wife to him, not making herself available. She did try time and time again for years, keeping herself looking good, even having a couple of cans for him at home and being pretty and sexy around him. She did it for the sake of the kids and she did like a bit of fun like every lovely feisty woman does. She didn't love him any more but she had a lot of time for him, he was the father of their three kids after all.

Mary was lucky to have her mother nearby who always helped out looking after the children when she could. She worked part-time in one of the few remaining grocery shops and in the chipper at weekends. There's no lack of work ethic and camaraderie in the inner city. There was also a complete acceptance of a man being an alcoholic, but an alcoholic woman was completely frowned upon.

Mary was still at school when she met Marty who was a few years older. They were a lovely young couple. Within months Mary was pregnant and everyone knew and were delighted with the news. All very accepting, no social snobbishness, it was kind of the norm in inner city, no judgement just support. The Church didn't have the same iron fist over the inner city folk as they did down the Country. In poorer areas life is a constant struggle and children would grow up quickly, get employment and help bring more money into the households.

By the mid nineties Marty was well 'on the soup' as people in the area politely called it. Mary knew any supports she got wouldn't rear the children. She was a bright young girl who got caught and she certainly didn't want her children falling into the same trap. In hindsight she would have and should have gone to England, America or even Australia, but sher she thought she had landed on her feet fair and square. What a mistake she made, but was very happy with her offspring. In order to make a few quid she joined a firm of contract cleaners doing offices, shops, banks and various other businesses around city centre. It was grand, not a bother, the money was ok and once you did a good job everything was grand. A few girls took a few shortcuts and they disappeared fairly quickly. Mary got plenty offers to go private but she was happy enough with the work and the company looked after all the taxes and insurance, so what she got into her hand every week she could keep. Eventually she was persuaded by a fine gentleman who owned three casinos and lived with his nice wife ten minutes away on a regular bus route from her, to come and work for him. He would put Mary on the payroll for the casino in town and give her cash for cleaning the house. She told him during the very informal interview that her husband was an alcoholic and she needed as much cash as she could get to feed and clothe the children. Her mam used to bring them shopping too and buy them jumpers and pants. For some strange reason she really opened her soul to this man who seemed really sympathetic to her circumstances. The hours were good too during school times and she didn't have to do weekends, as a couple of students did them. His wife worked part-time as a hairdresser and was really glamorous. They didn't have any children. It seemed on the surface to be a good move for Mary. She'd be up around forty quid a week plus the cash would come in very handy.

What followed was to be one of the most slippery, low life, conniving experiences for Mary. This fellow Peter was a real player and in hindsight Mary reckons his wife knew all about it and was happy to go along with it for the sake of her foreign holidays three times a year and her red sports merc as the second car. This was sleaze personified.

Peter let Mary alone for the first five or six weeks until she was totally dependent on her wages which were always paid by cheque, signed by him. He would drive her out in his Range Rover to the house on a Monday and Thursday and they'd be back for three when the children would be coming out of school. During the drives and the cup of tea outside sher you'd get to know a fella more and more. She liked Peter, he seemed a decent enough sort of skin and jaysus she got forty quid extra a week for those few hours.

It was the year after the Bill Clinton / Monica Lewinsky drama broke and more and more Peter would bring this up on their journeys out to the house. They would have the craic about it as everyone did at the time, a good few laughs, the odd suggestive remark and he'd ask Mary what she thought if it all. She said naively that it was only natural and joked about poor Bill being married to the ol' battleaxe Hilary, who was obviously more into political progression than making the breakfast, One of Mary's jobs was changing the bedclothes and freshening up the bedroom. Peter used to stay working in the office downstairs, which he started calling his Oval Office! It was all a bit cozy of a set-up and before too long there was the odd little hug which soon turned into a lot more. The cash improved as the weeks went by and his Oval Office became a twice a week blow job that increased Mary's take home cash by a further hundred quid a week. Mary thought sher what had she to lose and sher it was a bit of fun. Every Monday and Thursday it was straight into his Oval Office for what became known as a 'Clinton'. It was all pretty harmless really. She played it up and boy did he love it. He'd sit on the armchair and she'd climb all over him, a good french kiss and she'd slide down on to her knees, undo his belt, the button and slowly pull down his zip. Without too much more out it would pop through his y-fronts and she'd just teasingly touch the tip of her tongue to the top of his cock and tease, oh please he would say 'before its too late', she'd roll her lips and eventually her mouth around this big hard length of muscle and suck. Oh how Peter loved his 'Clintons'. The most powerful man in the world had his Monica and Peter felt as powerful in his little bubble with his Mary, but she would never go public, he was sure of that! It became like clockwork followed by tea and biscuits and a fairly rushed house cleaning operation. Peter started giving a hand stripping the bed and putting away the hoover and that sort of thing.

One day they went in Peter obviously had something else in mind, he held Mary's hand and headed towards the stairs with a sly smile. "No not now" she said as she definitely didn't want to get into a difficult situation, but really with the 'Clintons' the damage had started and it ain't going to get easier, quite the opposite. Within weeks Mary would say ok to Peter when she knew she was absolutely safe. They'd go upstairs into the bedroom and again it was all quite clinical, and yea she played well in her own feisty way, slip out of her clothes while he unceremoniously stripped off. There was a little foreplay, some kissing and soon he would catch his cock and not waste any time getting inside her and pumping all he'd got, without a thought for poor Mary who was really only thinking of the cash. Any day she was willing it was yet again another hundred quid, and on those weeks he'd help her a lot more, he'd even hoover the lounge.

For some reason one week they couldn't go out on the Monday and headed out instead unannounced on Tuesday. The red merc was there and the plumber's van. They headed straight for the kitchen when they went in and Mary started cleaning. The wife and the plumber came downstairs chatting loudly about the shower. Both had that dishevelled slightly bold look and ever so slightly embarrassed about fairly obviously being caught. It was at this stage Mary realised this was the norm for both in this house. Mary overheard the three briefly chatting about pipes n things and off with the plumber. The wife certainly didn't look as glamorous that day as she did in the photographs around the house. The total giveaway was that her hair and the plumbers hair were both recently quickly dried so they had either been at it in the shower or freshening up after the event. This house was without doubt a den of iniquity. Peter opened up one day and explained that they had a very open marriage, they couldn't have children so this was their way of keeping their lives exciting.

Everything was getting all too 'expected' for Mary or rather 'of' Mary. Her hubby Marty was causing her a bit of grief as he simply could not hold on to his job at this stage, drinking like hell and leaning on Mary for cash. This was happening over time while Peter was offering more and more for special favours. Mary was now in a catch twenty two situation with no way out, and yet she had this amazing bright outward attitude. But there was no light at the end of her tunnel. Her kids were fourteen, thirteen and nearly twelve, her mother was at her wits end with work and helping out. There were confirmations, Christmasses, birthdays, soccer matches, music lessons, cinema and on and on. Marty was a lovely ol' soul despite the drink, most of the time, and she had loved him once kinda. He got some sort of lump sum when he finished up at the brewery but that didn't last too long. He was a generous drunk in the pub and many took advantage of him. Despite all Mary's commitments she really wanted to pull back from her 'cleaning job' though oh god the money was good. The more she pulled back the more sleazy Peter reacted. He started holding back her pay cheques until all the 'housework' was done, he would up the cash element every now and again. She saw all the signs of more visitors to the house, and the odd time he was slow or unable to perform. His glam wife was away a lot more and he also was obviously drinking more and getting quite narky at times. This wasn't going to have a good ending, Mary had to get out. There was no easy way until one evening she picked up The Herald and hey presto there was a cleaning job advertised in the local Credit Union, where she had managed to put away a few quid, so they knew her in there. The money obviously wasn't quite as good and there were definitely no perks! She didn't need any references which was a major plus so suddenly on Friday after she got her wages and lodged them she went back to the casino to hand in her notice, well actually to say she was quitting straight away. She couldn't do another week. Luckily for Mary it worked out easier than she thought. The casino was busy enough at that time on a Friday evening so when she went in nobody took any notice of her. Up to the office with her and in the door fairly lively, a woman with a purpose. She was feeling very nervous. She hadn't a clue how Peter would react, as a man that's used to regular hanky panky cannot just turn off the tap. To her great surprise, though it shouldn't have been, there was Peter in the office with this young blonde, his hands all over her under her top, his belt buckle and top button undone and his trousers were beginning to fall off. Her hand was well down his y-fronts and giving him a right pull. Such was the passion they had neglected to lock the door. The blonde was a bit annoyed that some woman had barged in, while Peter was busily trying to pull himself together. For the first time he wasn't quite his confident cocky self, pardon the pun, and he blurted out "Mary, what are you doing here!?" With a wry happy confident smile, Mary who's nervousness quickly turned to shock and delight said "I'm here to tell you I'm leaving, I have another job." and then the feisty naughty Mary couldn't help herself saying "I'm glad you got a replacement." With that off out the door with her, Peter's mouth wide open, not a word he could say, and off trotted Mary with a spring in her step. That era was over. The timing of her resignation could not have been better!

Life is all about timing. The following day there was Mary on a damp afternoon on the side of a soccer pitch cheering on her little dynamo son Marty Junior or better known to everybody as just Junior. Usually he'd never miss a sitter of a goal like that but he seemed to have slipped slightly when he made contact with the ball. Junior knows every player in the Premiership in England and hopes one day to be playing for his favourite team Chelsea. He's a chip off the ol' block, a young version of Marty before the drink took hold. Marty senior also supported Chelsea, he loved soccer but now only on a television in a pub or where he was being dried out. He hadn't been to watch Junior play for a couple of years.

Graham on the other team, son of Jim and Joanne, shivered on the far wing, hated being there and would much prefer to be playing computer games at home, or down at Granny and Grand Da's with his Mum. The following year he would be going to boarding school anyway, and of course his mother would love him to play rugby and go on to become a solicitor. That's all she ever talks about as regards his career. It seems to be a given, or an obsession, in the legal world. On a soccer pitch in north inner city playing against a tough crowd poor Graham is like a fish out of water. On the other hand Jim feels totally at home. He grew up here, he recognises a few of the parents of the other team and he sees them in the supermarket which isn't too far away. The collection of people at the game is quite diverse, the cars in the car park from old and small to Joanne's new five series BMW. Jim never bothered getting a car as he didn't really need one. There's something about a man and a car though that is important, not just a status symbol or anything shallow like that, a car gives a man a certain confidence, but it has to be his car, not his wife's car. A motorbike doesn't do it, that only seems to solidify a mans low ranking in society, and oh god a bicycle is the last word. No woman ever ever wants to see her man on an ordinary push bike. It seems to be very much an Irish thing though as in Continental Europe most men and women seem to happily commute on bikes. We just prefer to clog up our cities with cars ticking over in traffic spewing out noxious fumes to choke everyone. The weather though plays a big part and now parking in town is a nightmare. Joanne is ok as her firm has an underground car park. Jim doesn't even like to be seen around these parts in a big mother fucker of a BMW, but Joanne couldn't really be seen driving into work in anything less.

Jim is doing a lot of thinking these days. When Graham was a younger child their world revolved around him, it was virtually every conversation, but now he spends most of his time in his bedroom, which leaves Jim watching television and Joanne reading over files or quickly and reluctantly doing some housework. Jim does his bit also. Its not hard to see now though that at this stage its not a happy functioning family. Jim never lost his lovely natural real inner city accent though it wasn't particularly strong, the supermarket was in a reasonably well to do part with plenty parking, and pretty much en route to wealthier areas, so a handy place to stop off on the way home for the professionals. Joanne on the other hand completely lost her midland accent when in the city, and it would only break out a little if she was on the phone to someone at home. Country people still and always would consider their original home as home and even if they spent most of their lives in the city it was always just considered functional accommodation.

Joanne was very good at just carrying on, being busy, smothered in work, she'd talk about it incessantly now that there was less Graham chat. Jim would listen away but would rarely comment. Was this rut going to continue indefinitely? Of course Joanne felt it too. Her only real friends were a couple of workmates as all contact with school friends was now well and truly gone. Holidays were even quite difficult for them as all lawyers congregated in only a few seaside villages, frequent the same pubs, get out their summer wear that they've had for the last twenty years, and all chat about the city and their favourite restaurants. Do these people actually live? They don't seem capable of mixing with any kind of ordinary folk. They vote conservative and hide away religious beliefs that they may have in case they would lose business over it. Jim dreaded these lawyer vacations and mostly he'd take off on his own and try to find some real local people in a lovely dark little pub with an open fire somewhere. The local farmers markets and the odd Church Fete were the only interesting gatherings they would attend as a family. As an only boy Graham was really truly lost. He had no first cousins on his mother's side and never met any on his father's side. They hoped that he would make more of a life for himself in boarding school and meet, as his mother would say, 'suitable friends'. Joanne's own mother was coming out in her, it was all back to how society would think of them all. Mostly Jim was fairly laid back about the whole situation but it was Joanne who seemed to be getting more and more dissatisfied with their marriage.

But of course nothing was said. Sometimes its better that way and if not forced things can work out in their own time in their own way. Speaking about counselling can be the beginning of the end as it confirms failure, from which there is rarely a satisfactory return.

Ironically Joanne did a lot of family law and had gotten a very good reputation. There was a lot of mediating between husbands and wives and more often than not unfortunately for all, except the lawyers, much court work, with couples tearing the hair out of each other.

Enter stage left, Bryan, a middle aged barrister, never married, a bearded bookworm who lived in his very smart sterile inner city mews apartment. He was good at his job with exceptional attention to detail with a habit of calming even the wildest attackers in court, a skill appreciated and loved by all judges to whom he afforded the highest respect. Joanne spotted this trait quickly and used Bryan a lot for her cases. Many a legal meeting and briefing took place prior to court appearances. Even if not on the same cases they would always go to lunch together when the court adjourned.

Bryan had this way of always catching a person by the arm, probably something he subconsciously picked up from a parent. At this stage Joanne and Jim virtually never touched or kissed or hugged each other anymore, their relationship had become very clinical. There was something about Bryan's arm touch that gave Joanne a warm tingle right up her whole body. For weeks and months they kept it all very professional but this couldn't last. They were getting on famously, laughing their heads off in Bryan's apartment over the smallest insignificant stories, which would bore the pants off most people. Once or twice she would test her relationship with Jim by repeating a story to which she would get virtually no response. She was using this knowingly to test out their relationship and their marriage. Oh she was having such fun with Bryan, they so spoke the same language. Some late briefings in his apartment involved ordering a pizza and cracking open a nice bottle of red. On these warm occasions juices and feelings in her body which she hadn't felt for years were re-emerging. As the pizza is shared and the wine is poured its sort of customary to have a toast and look into the other person's eyes. Oh god the connection! That dangerous moment when you realise this is special, this is different, a time when you realise almost immediately there ain't no turning back from this. You want to go along with it, you do go along with it, you pretend ah its only just having a bit of fun when in actual fact you'd love to be totally naked, easy and all over each other, not necessarily for sex only but for total and utter connection. You just want to jump in the deep end straight away. You wonder whether the other person is thinking the same way. You recoil in case its just your own fantasy, or a deep want within you. For the likes of Joanne and Bryan this was a relatively slow burn of slow burning kind of people but it was fairly obvious to both of them now that it was real. Does one retract and start revisiting the case at hand or does one actually admit to being interested by asking a few personal questions. Bryan plucked up a bit of courage and chose the latter. Gingerly he started by asking where she was from and a little about her parents and old family business, how she got into law, you know the usual stuff coming from a male romantic virgin. Joanne by now realising she was in a sterile marriage wasn't going to miss this opportunity, and sher it was all pretty harmless anyway. She spoke freely about her parents, the family menswear business, her younger brother Jamie, and lots more about her beloved father and her snob of a mother, but nothing, nothing about her husband Jim and young Graham for now. But Bryan couldn't help himself there were feelings within him now which were stronger than his professional ethics, and he was on his second glass of wine which was loosening him up a bit, so he continued his line of questioning. He wasn't used to this though, he was surprising himself. He went too far and started asking Joanne about her marriage and her son and ……yes a step too far for now because Joanne despite everything at home was a genuinely decent soul from a country catholic family. This is engrained in one's psyche from a young age no matter how much one might have strayed from it. She goes silent, uptight, monosyllabic, yes, no, grand, he apologised, she says there's no need, he tops up their glasses and they have cleared another hurdle and have gotten a bit closer. "This is getting a little dangerous Bryan" she says "I am thoroughly enjoying your company." "Me too" comes a swift reply. Oh god she thought 'should I, I want to, I mustn't, I should be honest with Jim first' but Bryan at this stage had her by the arm and was looking straight into her eyes intensely, more than lovingly, he was excited, he didn't know what was coming over him. Joanne felt it strongly, they couldn't help themselves. Together they fell into each others arms and the kissing started first a little on the back of the cheeks but soon it was full on lips, mouths even an attempt by the totally inexperienced Bryan with a bit of tongue. "Oh god we shouldn't" blurted Joanne before getting into her long lost excitable self and basically jumped on top of him, her eyes her face her expression her whole body now with an intenseness of wanting her new mate so badly. She hadn't felt this way for years. She thought she would never feel this way ever again. "Oh god Bryan I don't want to stop" she murmured aloud. The barrister still had a jacket and tie on his dry cleaned white shirt, corduroy trousers, very proper casual wear in his world. Joanne straightened herself, her eyes dimmed and darted upwards as she pressed forward her body into his. Her fingers started to take off his tie and top button. His hands cupped around the cheeks of her bottom, she was wearing a nice long dress. They both shuddered with sexual excitement, there was no turning back, she had to make all the moves undoing the rest of the shirt buttons to reveal an old style white vest above his rather hairy chest. "Oh god Bryan what are we doing?" she asked with no response, for once the barrister was lost for words. He was full on hard, something he hadn't really ever felt and oh boy he was feeling manly about it. They were on the sofa, there was no time to go anywhere, and best not in case they would lose the moment. Joanne unbuckled his belt and undid his trouser button, slid down his zip, and then followed the unceremonious, uncultured, standing up, him pulling down his corduroys and y-fronts and Joanne pulling down her knickers and whipping off her dress, and back on the sofa with the two of them, she helped him in with his moderate sized manliness and pushed and jigged and banged like she hadn't banged for years, her phone went off in the background, which she heard but ignored as she and Bryan engaged in the most beautiful coital connectiveness, she pushed and pushed, he was well inside her and totally in another world, one he never entered before, it continued for moments, minutes who knows but after what seemed like timeless she was roaring with excitement, and roaring, and shouting and banging she was full on and came while Bryan was experiencing the most amazing sensation ever as he gave his all inside her and after another jig of hers and a few more jacks of his all, they both fell into a calm satisfied state with quiet groans of 'oh gods' and 'wows' and 'oh my gods', 'oh that was incredible'. He shut his eyes, he was totally shagged, knackered, worn out completely, he couldn't move. He stayed within her until there was no point, but didn't want this moment to end. When they both 'came to' they looked into each other's eyes with a deep sense of happiness, neither were going to regret, in fact quite the opposite. Without words or even thinking both subconsciously wanted this together forever. So the clean up wasn't embarrassing, Joanne headed off to the bathroom, while Bryan slipped on his clothes roughly. Then more wine to celebrate their real connection. This was good, this was real, they both so wanted this. Joanne remembers her phone had rung so went to check it, it was Graham so she had the slightest tinge of guilt, but just would say she had it on silent while 'working'. Joanne asked Bryan directly at this stage as she knew everything was utterly mutual "Bryan, would you like us to be a serious item? If you would I will gladly finish up my already dead marriage. You don't have to answer now you know. And you do remember I have a twelve year old son!?" Bryan could hardly say no in his present trance of seventh heaven and agreed wholeheartedly. They could now talk like lovers and discuss absolutely everything. What is it about real sex that knocks all barriers straight away!

Joanne wouldn't hang about and would tell Jim within days and suggest a settlement, prepare a separation agreement and they would part pronto. She knew Jim would agree to this. Graham would be going to a fancy boarding school within months which would leave Joanne and Bryan very free to spend lots of time together in both their properties. Now this was handy she thought a city centre mews apartment near all of their work, a fine detached house in the leafy suburbs and a solicitor/barrister team! This had all the elements of a happy ever after story.

For the time being life had to temporarily get back to normal until it could change forever. Joanne returned home not looking too dishevelled but very much feeling it. That feeling when you know you've been naughty, you're still feeling the feelings in mind and body, she re-enters her house slightly flustered, holding files to give the impression that she's been working late, portraying an exaggerated level of business, to a slightly surprised Jim who was thrown down on the couch. But at this stage he was beyond surprise, or interest. It was Wednesday night and Joanne wasn't going to hang around, she knew exactly what she wanted but just to get her head around it all. Her only concern was how Graham would react, how would he take to his Dad not being around and Mummy in a relationship immediately with another man? He obviously felt the clinical atmosphere in the house. Though so many say how resilient children are who really knows how they are thinking, how they will react and what long term effects it may have on them? They say children of broken marriages often end up in broken marriages, but that does not necessarily have to be, you'd imagine it depends very much on why the marriage broke up and whether it was totally there in the first place. In this situation Joanne thought well herself and Jim got together rather precariously and quickly, it seemed the right thing to do at the time, though really they hardly knew each other, but she was carrying their child. One of her main considerations at the time of course was her parents and how they would react. Twelve years later they are both still alive and well, the shop died a death so there really was no point in keeping it on even if young Graham was remotely interested. Joanne's Dad retired and the premises is now leased to a bookie franchise. How country town highstreets have changed!

What was mostly going through Joanne's practical mind was her assets and of course Jim was really entitled to half of them. He could possibly insist on staying in the house more for Graham's sake than his own. She knew Jim was a reasonable man but not an idiot. He may look for his 'pound of flesh'. In round terms, considering she was going to inherit all of her parent's assets and cash, and her/their house was fully paid off at this stage she was worth well over a million, in fact nearer two. So her offer to Jim would have to be substantial. He had savings but in comparative terms he had nothing. They had kept their bank accounts separate, Jim had basically paid for all the shopping for the thirteen years, and would pay for hotels, restaurants and the odd holiday. Joanne paid off the mortgage and her car loans. She was wondering whether to offer Jim one hundred thousand or double that? Knowing Jim she thought he would be happy with the lesser figure if it was a clean separation and he had no ongoing payments whatsoever including Joanne paying for all of Graham's education, school and college. Or so she thought!

Its amazing how the practicalities of it all consumed her mind over the next couple of days and nights. rather than all the feelings Graham may have, not to mind Jim! However uneventful their marriage had become they did have some lovely times on holidays abroad and down the Country. It was literally the only time Joanne would switch off and really that only happened in late summer when the courts were not in session. Even if they went away at Easter or any other time of the year she could never forget about work and was always in contact with the office. Jim's heart used to drop if they met other lawyers while on holiday as she'd click into lawyer mode immediately, and take at least a day to click out of it again.

For a father to look out on a lawn where he spent hours kicking a soccer ball or doing a bit of putting golf balls is heart wrenching. A treehouse, a slide, an old tractor in the shed, his first bicycle bought with such joy one Christmas and the excitement of the opening, the adjusting of the saddle and the stabilisers. For a father to have all of these memories around outside will bring tears for decades at lonely times. Its like when that Harry Chapin song 'Cat's in the Cradle' comes on the radio for years to come every father wonders what more he should have done for his children or with his children, and now that they are growing up how much will they see of them. How much more should be done in marriages to keep the family together for the sake of the children and for the couple's own happiness. Could Joanne and Jim's marriage have been a much happier one, should they have gone to counselling? Why does work and career consume your life, and take over from family life? Surely rather than thinking of it as being the most important aspect of one's life we should only consider it as a means to an end for a better life rather than allowing it to sacrifice life itself. Is it a sign of selfishness, greed, ego, or is it really a sign of ignorance and stupidity to let work take over? So many people get the balance wrong. Most are brought up with the notion of studying hard, playing a sport or two, doing well, getting an education and having a really good work ethic. Does many a parent get wrapped up in this rut? Is it more a father thing than a mother thing? Do mothers think of their children's welfare and happiness so much more than fathers, or do fathers just do it in a deep and quieter manner? One thing for sure a separated father cries a lot in silence, an awful lot. Its a very lonely boy place to be. Is this what is ahead for Jim? How will he take it? Is Joanne thinking of Jim, no, hardly at all, she is in a new state of excitement about her new lover, and how much she should offer to Jim. She considers it all her estate.

Saturday morning comes and a very strange atmosphere is palatable. Little is said other than times for a soccer match that afternoon. Thank god for the radio playing away in the background. Joanne and Jim rustle around, eat a bit, until Graham as predicted heads off to his room.

"Jim" she says "we have to talk." "Oh jaysus" he says "what about?" And off she goes "listen I'm very sorry but I won't mince my words, I'll be straight with you. We haven't been having the most exciting marriage for years now, and I know that's as much my fault as yours." Jim wasn't aware that he had been at fault but hey guys do live a lot in denial of any self-wrong. He thinks to himself oh god she's going to want to start counselling, a programme worse than hell in his opinion. He certainly wasn't expecting her next line "I've met someone." What a final statement, suddenly her secret was revealed in the open, and there was no return. Their marriage was over. Nothing can ever be said to reverse that, or rarely anyway. Trust is everything, and that was broken. Obviously this was going on behind Jim's back. He was gobsmacked, but almost not surprised. What would he say? Whatever he blurts out couldn't be the right thing at this stage, and why should it be. A sudden mixture of emotions comes over him. "Who" he says "Doesn't matter" she says and adds "it's someone I work with, we have become very good friends." "Sounds like you have alright" he says getting a little cross and wanting to gain the upper hand in this most difficult of conversations. "Jaysus I wasn't expecting that. Things weren't that exciting but I didn't realise you were having an affair behind my back." A new Jim was emerging that Joanne had never seen, nor had he! "Jaysus thanks for telling me anyway." He went quiet for a while and continued "does Graham know?" "No" she says. "Have you thought about him?" he roars a bit louder and angrier. "Go easy Jim please, lower your voice or Graham will hear" and at that moment Graham appears "What's going on Mummy?

Daddy? What's going on, please tell me?" " You better tell him Joanne, tell him your big news." This isn't how Joanne had planned it but she had to deal with the situation, and turned directly to Graham "Listen love, Daddy and I love you very much and nothing in this world will ever change that. Its just that, well, we won't be staying together as a married couple." Jim interrupts "Mummy has met someone else." "Have you Mummy?" Graham asks in a shuddering voice trying to hold back his tears. "Well yes Darling, that's true", and with that Graham breaks down in tears, he couldn't hold it back and he runs to his room. "Well done Joanne" was not what she wanted to hear Jim say "you better go and explain things to him, we'll talk later." That had to be done, she followed Graham and spent most of an hour with him, hugging the poor little lad whose secure family life, however clinical it was, had just finished for good. This day was happening as his whole life was about to continue, time with his mother now, time with his father later going and coming from his soccer match. But that couldn't be, there's no way Graham could play a match that afternoon. Jim rang the trainer while Joanne was in with Graham. "Listen, I'm sorry but the young fella can't tog out this afternoon. The missus and myself are splitting up and he's just heard about it." "No bother at all mate I'm very sorry to hear that but listen thanks for ringing me and you take care of yourself ok. If there's anything I can do just tell me, right?" That truly understanding inner city camaraderie comes out loud and clear at times like this. Its not just words they really would do anything for each other. In this area people come first, careers are secondary, decent to the core they are.

Jim was fast coming to terms with the new reality. Things weren't great but they were stable. Jim enjoys an easy life and a certain routine. All of a sudden he realises this isn't his home anymore, or would she be moving in with the new fella, he presumed it was a fella! More than anybody's this is Graham's home, Joanne only bought it and Jim only married in. Whatever happens in Jim's mind Graham's feelings must be of paramount importance, his security, his comforts during this very turbulent part of a young person's life. Jim suddenly felt almost homeless, he had nowhere to call his home, nowhere to throw himself down in peace. He suddenly felt he was in a house where he was no longer wanted. 'I better get a flat fairly pronto' he thought 'jaysus the price of it!'

Joanne re-appeared as a cold grim steely figure with a purpose. The cosy cuddling time with Graham turned fast when she saw Jim, but emotions were everywhere, now though she had to remain stern. "Thanks for landing me in it" she started "he's alright now" she said making Jim feel sort of responsible for everything. "Right come on let's talk" she continued. They both knew this was no time for fighting and whatever was going on they both had and will always have respect for each other, as god knows they've been through a lot together. Solutions become pretty obvious, and immediate, Jim knew he had to go. Joanne starts up "Listen its all pretty new, yes I know this fellow for a while, he's a colleague, but we haven't been together much if you know what I mean" to which Jim replies "Jaysus I know what you mean alright." "I didn't want to be disrespecting you, I believe I am doing the right thing, and that's now where we're at" she says in a matter of fact way. So in good ol' throwback style Jim asks "well what do you want me to do, move out I suppose?" "Well I've had a little time to think about it" she says again getting the upper hand "if you'd like to go and get your own place I'll help out financially. Before you say anything we both know you have rights and we both know this house is in my name and I paid for it." "With a helping hand" Jim adds not letting her away with anything. "I was thinking if I take care of Graham's education, all of his boarding school and college I could give you a lump sum of say a hundred thousand to get you set up in a new place." Well this set Jim off, yes he was a calm kind of guy but that was because he had trained himself to be. He was passionate, fair, decent but by god he wasn't going to be had. He was fuming but managed to not let it completely explode "Will you g'way o' that where would I be going in the city with a hundred thousand to buy a gaff! If I hadn't met you I'd own my own place by now." They didn't have to go through who paid for what over the years, they both knew only too well. Joanne knew her offer was on the very tight side and at this stage was regretting starting so low, it was a bit of an insult and genuinely she didn't mean that. Needless to say though she was a skilled negotiator. Equally Jim knew there was no point in taking her on legally, lawyers stick together like glue and he could end up with nothing. "G'wan" he said "say a decent amount" not wanting to sound as if he was begging "and I'll pack my bags and get the fuck out of here. Just one rule though... nobody moves in here within the next couple of years while Graham is here. It's his home, and I'll come and take him out to matches etc as I always do, ok?" "Right so" she says knowing she is getting there and its nearly sorted "will we say two hundred thousand up front, and we'll call it a day?" The finality was so clear and startling. "Ok so" says Jim "I'll be gone in a few days. I'll move into the spare room tonight. I've rung the trainer and cancelled Graham playing this evening but himself and myself will head away somewhere anyway ourselves."

And that was it, marriage over, just like that! As break-ups go it was an easy one, all sorted within a couple of hours.

Jim headed into Graham's room "hey buddy I got you out of playing that match this evening, but com'ere to me lets go off somewhere, the two of us for the afternoon, ok son?" "Thanks Dad" came a very loving quiet reply fighting back the tears by avoiding eye contact. Jim was trying to be all ok about it but the minute he turned around he had that choked feeling when you just want to burst out crying but can't be seen to do it anywhere, except when you're on your own in your flat, thinking about the times you had when he was a little one growing up. Gut wrenching stuff. He wanted to add 'will we go around one', but he knew he couldn't say another word without breaking.

Jim just had to get out of the house for a while on his own, so he wandered off down to the shop for the paper, another handy 'prop' to hide behind at a time like this. He thought he better start looking for a flat, rent or buy, something anyway, rent to start with he supposes until he gets his cash and organises a mortgage. As he heads out he feels some little sense of freedom, he starts to have those first very initial thoughts that he has a whole life ahead of him, that it was pretty stifling living with Joanne, and the thought of having his own place ain't too bad at all!

Then starts his own appraisal which gets very depressing. Maybe he was fairly hard to live with, as he was just an ordinary guy with an inner city accent, working in a local supermarket for oh god over twenty years now, and apart from being away on a few holidays he had never really been anywhere. He hadn't even been to too many places in this Country! Maybe, he thought, now's his chance, maybe himself and Graham could go away on a few holidays. Maybe he just wasn't exciting enough for Joanne, though god knows she wasn't too sociable herself, was he not intelligent enough for her, maybe couldn't have long conversations about international affairs or the history of the world, or something. She could but only in a very conditioned way, and only with her peers who all thought the same, or at least were taught to all think the same. He was trying to figure out why their marriage was so stale. In the beginning they had a bit of craic, but only really when they were alone, just the two of them together. The first year was all hiding the fact that Joanne was pregnant, they even managed to keep Graham's birth secret to get another month out of it and blamed all sorts of things so as not to bring him down to her elderly parents for another month after that. Was all that secretive stuff always playing on Joanne's mind, Jim didn't really care, he was as proud as punch to have a young son. Oh god he thought that will be another huge shock for Graham some day when he realises his actual birthday is a month earlier and the penny drops. How will he take that, it probably wouldn't arise until he's applying for college.

Joanne always tightly holds on to his passport, he's never had it in his own hand.

Can an aspiring lady solicitor mixing with all her aspiring colleagues be married to a shop boy in charge of the veg!? Did he always find it difficult, but never said. She rarely brought him to anything work related, even Christmas parties. Was he what you'd call a 'token husband'?

Jim took the long way around by the park to go to the shop, he needed this extra time, and its nice at times like this to be in some sort of nature, I guess its about getting back to basics, reality, and trying to understand everything from there. Should he not have proposed that day, should they have waited to have the baby first and just been straight with everyone? Would it have killed Joanne's father as she thought it might, or would he have just gotten over it? God maybe he should have gone to night courses and become something, maybe a quantity surveyor or some kind of an architects technician or something, and maybe changed jobs, built up a new career for himself, but it wasn't too easy with the different shifts he had to do, and often had to switch shifts at a moments notice. If he read more intellectual stuff like history or developed a big interest in cars or something, anything, though he did enjoy photography, maybe he should have done photography courses. Jim just lived, but loved it. He went for his few pints, went to the odd match, supported Man U, went to work, and was one hell of a really nice guy to everyone he met. He wasn't that opinionated about anything special and just mostly agreed away with whatever anyone was on about. He just liked their company, a few laughs, a bit of craic, sher you know yourself.

That's how he came across but there was another Jim that few knew about, the deep thoughtful passionate generous Jim who remained unnoticed. He could never pass a person on the street without putting a few decent coins in his or her container, never passed a musician on the street without throwing something in, he very often donated to charities in the city, he hated to see anyone cold or hungry, his kind heart reached out to them, and he could never see his mother short, even if it was for drink. His background shaped his character, he didn't want for material things but always careful and terrified really of ever falling back into poverty, as he knew how hard it was to rise out of it, especially as you get older.

Though he never mentioned it losing his sister that time to drugs upset him very deeply. He saw her progression from having the craic with her mates to being proud of being part of the 'hip' gang. She got off with one of the main guys who dressed well, spoilt her with jewellery and nights out, he had a fancy sports car, black of course, and she looked well in the passenger seat. Jim saw her decline. He came across her on the street langers drunk and drugged a few times, helped her home on numerous occasions. He loved her, he cared deeply for her, but he couldn't do anything for her, and often wondered afterwards that maybe he could. That guilty feeling remained with him. He has seen so so many like his sister in the city, they sometimes come into the shop just to walk around to get warm. He has been known to buy stuff he's seen being shoplifted rather than make a big issue of it. He'd just quietly leave a few quid with one of the girls or guys on the till and direct the person towards that one. Jim had huge respect for all, well maybe more for the less well off, his own.

Did he propose out of kindness, practicality or for a good life? When everything got really mundane should he have moved on? He had his chance with his imaginary lover Maag one night. Both were finished the late shift and Jim was locking up, putting all the cash in the safe, there were a few cleaning up around the shop but it was just himself and Maag in the office and oh christ was she looking well at the end of her shift. There was definitely chemistry there, and she was well up for it. If it hadn't been for timekeeper at home, and he had her car that night. Even if it had been a Saturday night when he could have stolen a little of his drinking time to be with this buxom beaut, oh god she had amazing ride written all over her face. She was really winding Jim up with suggestive questions, body movements, ran her hand down his leg, sat up on the desk "would you like to Jim, I would, I'm feeling so horny right now." "Oh my god Maag jaysus I would in a shot, you're fucking gorgeous, to be honest I've wanted to for years." "Goooood" she says "lets do it, my place?" There would be no hanging around with Maag. "Oh jaysus I'd love to Maag, but I can't, I have to go home, sorry." His sexual fantasy was dashed, Maag moved on swiftly, and Jim never got another chance, except imagining it in the shower. Just once he thought, just once.

Oh how the mind can beautifully wander on a walk down to get the paper on a sunny Saturday morning, even after a marriage break-up! Isn't imagination amazing, a great escape from reality, at anytime you let your mind go there.

Jim needed more time to himself so stopped and sat on a park bench on his way back with the paper. He opened up the page with apartments for sale and to let. Having browsed at a few his world suddenly fell in again and he couldn't stop his eyes welling up and a few tears escaping. This was going to happen so many times especially on the big occasions. Its not just a marriage break-up, or knowing your ex was seeing someone behind your back and probably sleeping with them. Even if the big love isn't there anymore, there's still and always will be some love, after all they did spend many years together full of memories and most importantly shared their love and DNA in their most precious being of all, their son. And its not only just that, you get very used to the security of being in a house, a home, its a whole routine that doesn't have to be thought about, and there's space, lots of space in the big detached house with a huge lawn out the back, in a nice area in the leafy suburbs, with parks and trees and ponds and people you recognise and share a smile or a little chat with, a 'Happy Christmas', Easter, 'lovely day', or complimenting on each other's offspring as they grow up. Missing all of this is heart wrenching, the routine of it all. Through his wet eyes he spots some apartments to let, there's a nice one-bedroom in the city centre, near where all city transport hubs are, with underground parking, fairly pricey but ok for what it is and that area. He rings the number and hey presto the phone is answered and it turns out to be privately owned and he arranges to view it on the next day, Sunday. A little bit of positivity amongst life's present turmoil. On the upside what man doesn't like to have his own cave!?

The afternoon will be the most emotional of his life. Pulling himself together Jim returns in home, eyes dried but obviously so. You always know when someone has been crying, and Jim never did cry. Joanne could sense it as could Graham, the atmosphere was quiet and sombre. "C'mon so son we'll head off" he said as he grabbed the keys of Joanne's beamer for what might be the last time. Off out to the coast with them in silence trying to keep back their manly tears, not able to speak. The odd few words about what station to listen to on the radio. Beaches are lovely but why do we always head for them when we are sad, for those long lonely walks. Its good to hear the waves lapping and feel the chilled cleansing breeze on the face. Jim and Graham walked down the strand, Jim threw his arm around his twelve year old and just couldn't hold back the tears anymore. "Its ok Dad, it'll be ok." To Jim's huge surprise and its something he will never forget for all his living days his son comforting him as he broke down. Who could ever realise the strength and mature understanding of a twelve year old! He was minding his Dad and making sure he was ok. They couldn't chat about what was in their minds, about who Mummy had met, how long was it going on, did either know or suspect anything, it was too early and raw for all of that. Or when Jim would be moving out or where would he go? But one thing had to be said however as difficult as it was for Jim "Graham you know myself and Mammy love you beyond everything else in the world and both of us will always be there for you" oh he had to take a breather "you know you can contact me any hour of the day or night, and hey no secrets ever ok!?" Through the quiet tears of Graham came "Ok Dad", "Promise?" "Promise!" They will both learn in time that of course communication is difficult, so much more can be said and felt when together, texts and phone calls are ok but for a teenage boy and his Dad it can be hard enough to make conversation. At least Jim will be living near enough so he can bring Graham to his matches. But all that will change in September when Graham heads off to boarding school. The mood lifted when Jim said "I've decided to buy a car!" "Cool Dad, what kind?" "What kind a one would you like, you decide!" "A Golf, they're class." "Ok lets swing by the Volkswagen dealer on the way home to have a look." That meant so much more than just a car to Graham, it meant his Dad could pick him up any time, bring him places, for just a spin or collect him from boarding school. Graham thinking ahead said "you might teach me how to drive Dad will you?" "Of course, now there's a great idea!" Their bond was strengthening already, their future together looking a whole lot brighter, planning things they could do together. "Hey, then we could hit for the West, try some surfing or golf or something" Jim said with a smile breaking out. This time together was more than vital, deeply comforting despite being highly emotive. They needed to be together, be quiet together, cry together, laugh, smile, plan, love each other, and put in place a very firm unspoken pact for the future. And all in a few hours. Graham was already having to start growing up fast, he would become more independent and self-assured sooner than others. Its a lot to put on a twelve year old, and not something a parent necessarily considers when having an affair. Maybe there's an upside for a child, or maybe it takes from enjoying their childhood. In the weeks and months to come he would miss his day out, get very lonely, be stuck more with babysitters, wonder where his Mum is and who she is with, when he would have to meet his new 'step-dad' and what he'd be like? There will be a lot of anger, sadness, even guilt when he even wonders whether he was to blame. Whatever is planned and is said Dad was leaving home and things would never be the same again. That's an awful lot to put on the shoulders of a child. If a marriage is only just ok should parents always put their children first and not attract new friendships, relationships, sexual encounters with others for their own selfish indulgences. How good, bad or boring does a marriage need to be to make such adulterous dalliances ok? Is it easier for the better well off, harder for the struggling household, or does it make any difference? We are all basically animals at the end of the day, with less loyalty, some self-respect and meant to have a higher intellect. Sometimes you'd wonder when the people's behaviour takes precedence over the lives of their offspring. The latter remain much loved but often feel less important. Should parents in a loveless marriage forego the opportunity to love again, to be in a new happy relationship, to live again, or should they remain in a heartless household? What would be the better option for the children? Jim and Graham might not, well will not, see as much of each other but their times together will be very special. Home will be a quieter place for a good while as Jim's only request was that the home remains just their home and no new fella can move in for the foreseeable future. In other words Joanne can 'fuck off' and meet her new lover elsewhere!

They drive to the Volkswagen garage, its still open, Graham gets to pick the car, the colour, go for a test drive in the fabulous black Golf GTI, five door. Hey he thought things are definitely looking up!

"Hey Mum Dad bought a new car" Graham blurted with excitement as he tore in the door "he's picking it up next week, she's a beauty and I got to sit in the drivers seat and turn it on." The competition had started, one nil to Jim! Immediately she wondered how she will be able to do exciting things with Graham. Now she's also committed to time needing to be spent with Bryan, more shopping and cooking, more housework, more driving Graham to and from school, and unfortunately he wasn't a kid who had started sleepovers. What has she done!? Her afternoon phone call with her new beau while the lads were out was a little less exciting than she had thought it would be, all ok its just that Bryan was one of those confirmed bachelors who read a lot in his incessant avarice for knowledge. And he hasn't told her he snores, bigtime!, which he is a little worried about.

"Supper's in the oven" Joanne says "I'm heading out" leaving the two guys to have a really lovely night in now that things had already begun to settle. A definite own goal for Joanne. Two nil to Jim! She returned from her pleasant evening at the mews to find the two lads fast asleep in Graham's big double bed.

Jim slipped away early Sunday morning and got breakfast in town before viewing the apartment at eleven. It was perfect, not only the actual apartment overlooking the river, only fifteen years built, a lovely area, but also owned by a retiring lady teacher who had recently headed back to her country parish. Perfect for Jim and perfect for the landlady who really wanted to let it long term to a nice single person who would mind it as she did. Over coffee in the nearby café she even agreed to give Jim first option if she was ever selling it. She had gotten dozens of calls for it she said but had a nice feeling about Jim after their little chat on the phone. Fully prepared she brought two leases and luckily Jim's cheque book was in his jacket. Deal done, deposit paid, all signed up and he could move in immediately, sorted!

There's a finality about packing most of your clothes and personal belongings, and an urgency about getting out of somewhere where you are now treated as a visitor. How quickly everything changes. Luckily when Jim returned to what now was his old home Joanne and Graham had gone to the cinema, she was trying not to lose too much ground. Jim furiously packed taking his opportunity to do it in peace. He threw all his clothes into a few cases, a few bedclothes in refuse sacks, his mug, his bathroom stuff, his camera, a few books he considered his, a photo of Graham from the mantlepiece, and all of a sudden he looked at a heap of bags in the hallway which he realised was all of his worldly belongings. After calling a taxi, he had a good look around, he grabbed a sheet of paper and an envelope and cried his eyes out while writing a note to Graham which he left on his bed. He apologised for slipping away but explained that he couldn't do it any other way. He'd see him on Saturday for the next match, and asked him to look after Mammy. With all his love and floods of tears he closed the envelope. He took off his wedding ring and placed it on Joanne's dressing table.

It wasn't the first time the jovial taxi driver was in this situation. He also was a city boy and couldn't have been more supportive to Jim who at this stage was totally broken. Leaving your home and family is one of the hardest things life will ever throw at you. Arriving at a new apartment, throwing everything in and going to the nearby shop for milk and bread and a few other provisions is one of the most sobering experiences a person will ever feel. All of a sudden there you are thrown down on a new couch staring at the four walls, totally alone.

In life you really have to reach rock bottom to see the light, learn the lessons, reset your mind and rise up stronger than ever, but when you're down there its hard to see that. Financially Jim is ok but emotionally he's totally wrecked, deflated, feeling old, drained and totally alone. Thinking of his boy opening his note on the bed breaks his heart, he just had to write something to him, not just be gone without a word. Thank goodness for work the following day to get him back to some normality, some structure. He rang Graham on Monday evening, his little voice was so quiet, quivering at times. Jim just had to take breaks and go silent or he'd be gone again. It was like suddenly not being able to breathe. There were lots of these phone calls at the start but they got fewer and fewer as time went on. Whenever they met up though they both felt the depth of their love and connection, but every time leaving was heart breaking.

Little did Jim realise as he sat there alone at night that this apartment was going to be the happiest place of his life, that he was going to meet the love of his life, and in fact he had already met her!

Saturday came and Jim rocked up to his old home in his super duper black GTI. Joanne gave a wry smile thinking that she paid for that but she couldn't say anything. She had another little bag of his stuff that she had picked up around the house all ready for him. Graham shot out with huge excitement, jumped into the drivers seat, his face beaming and just thrilled to see his Dad again. "C'mon son, get your gear and we'll head off."

It was the second leg return match of the league. The lads took off in great style with a bit of revving going on for extra effect. The weather wasn't great but it didn't matter the mood was of total temporary happiness. What a rock n roll week it was!

Togged out and on the pitch Graham was with his team. The trainer nicely spotted Jim and came over for a friendly chat, not mentioning anything but checking all was ok. Inner city folk have an innate skill in counselling at the highest level, without needing any training or qualifications, just experience in the university of life, the best of all.

Jim was a bit 'out of it' after one of his most difficult weeks when he suddenly heard this familiar voice roaring "G'wan Junior, go for it." Junior had scored and she jumped around with delight cheering at the top of her voice, and right at that moment again her eyes caught Jim's and neither wanted to part. "Oh jayz hi'ya", "how'ya. Good goal! He's a dinger, is he your fella?" "Yea he's great, he lives for it. You from around?" "I've just moved into town, but I work in Treacy's." "Oh right, d'ya know I was never in there, always thought it might be a bit expensive." "No, we've great ol' offers, you should try it sometime." "I will, enjoy the match."

That's as much, in fact probably more than society allows strangers of the opposite sex to chat, but oh the sense of friendliness and positive vibes between them was palpable. They caught each others eye many more times during the match, and a little wave as they were leaving.

She couldn't wait to go to Treacy's but managed to wait until Tuesday afternoon after work. There he was, smart as a soldier, confident as a lion, in charge of his jungle of vegetables. She crept up behind him and said kind of cheekily "any ol' offers there mister?" Jim turned in delight recognising the accent "Oh jays how'ya? First time in the shop!" "Yea its a fine shop, much bigger than I thought. Did ya enjoy the match? even though we beat yous" she said with a naughty laugh. The fun and banter was starting. They couldn't really spend all day chatting here so he took the bull by the horns in his new found freedom and without really thinking blurted out "would you like to go for a drink sometime?" "I can't really be seen out, if ya know whar I mean, there's no problem, I'll explain another time, but yea I'd love to meet up." With that Jim tore off a bit of cardboard off one of the vegetable boxes and put his number on it and handed it to her "Jaysus I don't even know your name, I'm Jim." "I'm Mary." "It's lovely to meet you again Mary, hey come over to my new gaff, if you don't mind that is, its on the quays." "Ok, I will." The real inner city directness had come out again, she continued "ok so I better get a few things and head off to pick up the kids, I'll see ya" she said holding up the piece of cardboard as if it was a winning lottery ticket. She minded it with her life and texted that night. And so it began.

About Mary

Thursday night seven o'clock Mary had her mother in childminding, all fed, and she was trying to do herself up without it looking too obvious. She told them she was just meeting a friend and she might be late. Her long coat covered the pretty flowing dress she was wearing. Mary intended to impress. Jim was fairly organised as he got cover at work for the afternoon. He bought a couple of nice steaks, as she said she liked meat, He had all the trimmings, onions, sauce, spuds, peas, the lot. Loads of red and white of different types just in case she had particular favourites. The apartment was reasonably clean, fresh towels in the bathroom, a few candles lighting, oh god for both of them it was so exciting! Nervous, yes, very but a confident nervousness. Neither had been on a real date for many years. Mary hung around a nearby shop, picked up a bottle, she was early, but she still worried that she might not find his place, but not a problem. Jim had given her the code downstairs and she made her way up to the third floor, shaking with excitement at this stage. Jim was checking everything for the umteenth time, looked at himself in his smart casuals in the mirror and 'here goes' the doorbell rang and he opened up. Their eyes met like they always meet, in she came, and Jim opened his arms and in she went for a lovely close hug. They separated a bit and she said "oh god I needed that, I haven't felt so nervous for years." They both knew the best way was just to be normal "Lovely place, you haven't been here long, have ya?" "Since Sunday week" Jim replied "What!" and they both laughed their heads off, a great ice breaker. "I've a lot to tell you" Jim said. "Oh god that makes two of us" she replied with a laugh and added "we'll make it a competition who can shock who the most." They wined and dined and wined and laughed and chatted and held hands like teenagers on the couch. They both felt extremely comfortable. One still married, the other separated since Saturday week, but she didn't know where her husband was, he'd been gone for a couple of weeks. Poor ol' Marty he comes home now and again. "You're only separated since Saturday week, jaysus you're a fast mover!" she laughed, they both did. He explained all, she understood completely. Neither of them had come down in the last shower. Jim explained a little about the heartache of leaving his son "C'mon give's a hug" Mary said to console him, she could feel his loss. They had the nicest little hug and stayed very close to each other. This was pure heaven, there was not a doubt in the entire world that these two were complete soulmates. There was no way this was just going to be a once-off. They were in super form together. "I better be heading away" Mary said around half ten/quarter to eleven. "Ah no" says Jim wishing the night would never end. At this stage they had consumed a couple of bottles, had lovely steaks and stuff and were well into the third bottle. They had made an agreement to be totally open with each other. Both of them knew they couldn't be seen out together, but what the heck it didn't matter. Jim's apartment block was full of transient financial services types of various nationalities and it was a world apart from either of their homes while at the same time only about ten minutes away by taxi.

"I'd love you to feel totally at home here Mary." "Ah that's lovely, you know I already do." "Will you come around again soon, anytime" Jim says "I'll always have some food here for us, you know pasta n stuff." "Are you around Saturday?"

Mary asked "maybe around eight again?" "Yea definitely, super." She had to go but it wasn't so bad now that they would see each other again within forty eight hours. Jim called a taxi, went down with her and just slipped the taxi driver a twenty with a wink, a gesture in inner city language meaning 'say nothin', keep the change'.

Mary got home and she and Jim spoke on the phone for at least a couple of hours. There was a very smiley person cleaning the Credit Union on the Friday and a very happy guy in charge of the veg in the supermarket. Rushing home on Saturday he had to prepare the place for his fabulous new friend. Sunday was the day he got to see Graham this weekend, and he was on a high!

Saturday night came and our new loving couple were well loved up, this was real, having a lot of fun, lots of conversations from the deepest level to the sublime, full of chat, full of chemistry. The music went on and our couple took to the floor to dance a lovely slow one. This is one of the occasions where neither want to go too fast and spoil everything but at the same time they both know there was no spoiling what they felt for each other already. But the music was on and the lights were dim and they were so close they were inhaling each other "Oh god Jim this is amazing" Mary said quietly "how did we get to meet each other, is this just a dream?" "Well lets not wake up if it is" Jim replied "let's stay in our dream." I'm all for that you gorgeous hunk" she couldn't help it she was beginning to feel very horny "I'm totally comfortable with you Jim, I want to stay in your arms." Jim wasn't great at the mouth talk but he sure wasn't slow with the body talk. He pressed himself into Mary when she realised he was feeling the same. They gently rubbed noses back and forth and ventured the slightest contact kiss on the lips, so slow, so romantic, so sensual "Take me to the moon if you want" she said. This was going to be slow as they both wanted to savour every moment and treat each other with the utmost respect because this was real, this was incredible. "Can I touch you Mary." "Oh yes anywhere you want baby, anywhere you want." He put both hands on her neck gently and they kissed stronger and stronger, she had her hands around his lower back and pressed herself hard into him, one hand coming around the front to the buckle of his jeans which she just held for a while. The music played, the candles glimmered, and Jim brought his hands under her top and onto the bare skin front and back. As she undid his belt and top button she lowered her hand down and around his cock, which she now considered hers, all hers. Jim undid her bra at the back with ease and started fondling her beautiful well formed breasts, her nipples were erect with anticipation. They wanted to be part of each other so bad, they wanted to be one, this was going to be so much more than just sex. "I'm yours Jim" Mary murmured "I'm yours." His jeans fell and she helped his boxers down, her beautiful long slinky skirt had only elastic holding it up above her nickers of pure silk. Shoes off and whatever clothes from the waist down slipped off nicely. She held him so that he touched into her vulva, just a little, he rubbed her breasts and kissed her lips, oh they so wanted this to last forever. Mary had the most beautiful petite but strong body which was more like a twenties than early forties, so well shaped. Jim was a hunk, a real man, strong, passionate, big hands making her feel oh so comfortable and oh so safe. They moved slowly over towards the couch, he helped her down and he fell to his knees and rubbing her body up and down, reaching up to kiss her and slinking down to lick her hard with his tongue deep in where she loved it most making her groan with lust "oh come inside me Jim, come inside me." It was all Jim could do to wait for the call and he duly obliged, straight in slowly and with utter feeling further and further in to her groans of contentment and a little "uh" and "ooh" whenever she twitched inside with sexual excitement. All the way in and moving a little in and out and until both were really and truly coming together. It seemed he was in further than was ever possible at this stage. They moved slowly with the odd jerk for ultimate penetration and "oh god" and then the real magic took over and they both were in full unison at full sexual connectiveness both groaning louder and louder and "oh god, oh god Jim, come, come, and Jim was giving his all with all his manliness he came hard and strong within her with a final push and a big deep roar "oh god, oh god" and then the slower quieter "oh gawd, oh Mary, hmmmmmm, wow, oh my good god Mary that was the most incredible." "Mother of god you're good Jim, oh god you're good." They just rested there without moving for some time just feeling what they were feeling, total togetherness, this was total loveliness, nothing in the world compares to this. They were so together. He rubbed her breasts gently a little more and they slow kissed for ages until that moment when both realise that was amazing and that's it, over for now with those feelings forever. "that's the couch baptised anyway" Mary says. "We'll just have to work our way around the apartment" Jim replied with a naughty husky little animal like response, both laughing and so on the same page. "I'll grab a couple of towels there and stick on the shower" Jim says. Their loving kissing and feeling each other continued over their warm soapy bodies as they showered together. They were completely all in to each other, this was just incredible. Back on the couch all clothed up, cozy and snugly they sipped their wine, chatted and had that true post lovemaking relaxed happy feelings. "Well are we lovers now?" Mary asked. "We're most definitely lovers now, after that, my god" Jim replied with a smile. "We're both kinda married though aren't we?" she said. "Yea, kinda" Jim replied and they both broke down with laughter. "I love that, you don't give a shit do ya!" she laughed. "Not in the slightest" Jim said "and it's so nice being together here on our own with nobody bothering us, or having to talk to anyone." "Will we get fed up of just being here and not going out?" Mary asks, and he says with a smile and a wink "what d'you think?" and they both break down laughing again "anyway sher can't we go to exotic places together and keep this place as our own private paradise. God what people wouldn't give for this". "Our own secret hideaway, our love nest, feck the rest of the world, we have our very own world here."

And so these two lovebirds welded together in absolute secrecy, and so it continued, for weeks and months, and years. Jim never told Graham, Mary never told her three. To Jim's delight Mary became pregnant, and even though Marty came home now and again he'd be so out of it he actually thought he was the father! Mary and Jim lived very happily as part-time secretive 'husband and wife'. It was just too perfect to change. They both kept their jobs, Jim's paid a lot more being management so he would just put a little envelope in Mary's bag every weekend. Jim met Graham most weeks but less and less as the years rolled on and he headed off to college. They had a good relationship. They would rarely talk about Joanne, Jim just made sure all was ok at home and always gave Graham a few quid. The only time he met the new fella Bryan was at Joanne's fathers funeral, they were all polite. Graham travelled with Jim to it and they left early enough. Graham still had an inner anger and said of Bryan 'He ruined everything' to Jim's reply 'there were two of them in it.'

Mary anyway had a big bouncy baby boy which they called Brendan. For the first few months while breastfeeding she would bring young Brendan to the apartment, which was at this stage very much their apartment, Mary kept a load of clothes there and had personal stuff all over the gaff. As soon as Brendan was on the bottle she would leave him with her mother who almost reared him. It was great company for this ageing spritely granny. Mary's older three headed to their friends in Australia more or less as they all hit eighteen or finished school. There was a right little bunch of locals from the area together out there, all working hard, all doing well, and meeting up with loads of Irish culchies from all over the Country. It broke Mary's heart when young Junior took off, they were always so close. When they were all gone Jim and Mary went on their one and only holiday abroad together, her Mam looking after young Brendan. They booked off-season, separate seats on the plane on the off-chance there would be anybody they'd know on the flight. They had picked a fairly fancy hotel in Portugal in a place they had never heard of, a good long way from the busy spots. Their secret remained safe, though it was a bit of a chance to take. Oh what fun they had, they wined and dined and swam and fell in love with cocktails. They called it their honeymoon, took loads of photographs and made everlasting memories. A trip of a lifetime.

Brendan grew up to be a fine young lad, cute out but not really academic. A good job came up in the stores at Treacy's during the first covid lockdown. Brendan applied for it and miraculously got it! He'd meet Jim very often every day as he checked in stuff from all the delivery trucks and vans and helped Jim and others load it up for the shop. He was super at his job, everyone got on with him. He was one of those guys that would do that bit extra for you always. Himself and Jim hit it off famously. Mary's other three couldn't travel home with the travel restrictions and all as Australia was very tight on that but they managed to see lots of each other on zoom calls, probably more chatting than if they were all living together, but it wasn't the same.

The memories, the years had all drifted into each other. Jim and Mary's life together was different, but it was theirs, and they loved it. Back a few years Mary had a little cancer scare but thankfully nothing too serious, something removed and a bit of radiation, all clear thank God.

Their reality was suddenly jolted back into the present as Mary's face went from her beautiful smile to a grimace of agony. Some pain had happened in some part of her body and it hurt her, but she wasn't leaving just yet. She knew Brendan was on the way. Jim clasped her hand even tighter to make sure she knew she wasn't alone. It had all happened all too quickly, only weeks before she had her vaccination for the wretched old virus, as she thought she better, working in the Credit Union and all. Soon after her cancer came back and ravaged through her body so fast. Several people in the locality had similar experiences and there seemed to be funerals every day. It was too late for treatment, it was so rapid. Jim didn't know whether he was coming or going, the love of his life, and Jim hers, without a shadow of a doubt. There they were nearing the end of their secret lives together, so so lucky to have met each other way back on the side of that soccer pitch on that damp Saturday afternoon. What a beautiful couple for the two decades they had together.

With that the hospice bedroom door opened and in came Brendan. He stopped "Jim, how come you're here?" It was all too much to process in that moment with his mother dying in the bed. "Come on over Brendan, pull up a chair and hold your mother's other hand, she will want to know you are with her." Brendan pulled up the chair and took her hand in his. On the bed was a fairly tattered photograph album. Mary still had her eyes closed but Jim felt she was listening. Brendan looked at his Mam in pain and felt every bit of it shivering down his own body. Then again he looked over at Jim and just couldn't for the life of him understand why one of the managers from Treacy's was holding his mother's other hand, but he felt the kindest warmest most

lonely boy

comforting feelings coming from the other side of the bed. Jim with his other hand pulled up the photograph album to over Mary's stomach and he started to open it, Brendan was watching though still completely at a loss. The first photo was of Mary at a table, wine glass in hand looking so young, exuberant, and happy, it was Jim's favourite photograph of her. He turned the page and there she was glowing with a hand on her pregnant tummy, and onto the next page a little baby on her front covered in blue and white. Jim flicked through the pages showing all the photographs. There were a few of Jim but not many, and lots of Brendan growing up, loads of Brendan at school, his first day, to the Christmas concerts, on the soccer pitch, ones with his granny, loads with Mary and the penny was beginning to drop and Brendan's eyes welled up. There were plenty empty pages towards the end but Jim went to the inside back cover where there was the most beautiful photograph of Jim and Mary enjoying their cocktails in their hotel in Portugal. "We asked the waiter to take this one" Jim said quietly to Brendan. "So you're my Dad?" Brendan gulped. "Yep I sure am son, and I couldn't be more proud" Jim said "your Mam and I lived the most beautiful secret life anyone could ever imagine." Jim reached across for Brendan's other hand which was forthcoming without hesitation. Mary's eyes opened and she and Brendan looked at each other, mother and son, intently and without words transferring all their love. She looked over at Jim and smiled. "Don't worry Mary I'll look after our Brendan, and sher I'm sure he'll keep our secret." A total happiness came over Mary's face, she knew her son was going to be looked after by the kindest man in the world. She closed her eyes with all their hands connected, her pain disappeared in a room of love as she passed with ease of mind into the great unknown.

The End

lonely boy xx

About Jim

by lonely boy

Dedicated to
The LOVE of *MY* LI*F*E

What was it about Mary? Jim continually wondered through his uncontrollable grief. He sat at the back of the Cathedral as if he had just happened upon Mary's funeral mass. He kept his composure sitting there dressed casually in his civies. It is so hard to be close to people at a funeral but not being able to be together with the grieving family. There was his son Brendan the main man with cousins and Mary's poor mother beside her coffin. Jim went to holy communion so for one last time he could be within a few feet of Mary as he walked past. The photograph on top was the beautiful one he took of Mary so happy holding her wine glass, the one from the front of their photograph album. Jim had taken it on the one and only holiday they had away together in Portugal. He lent it to Brendan who had put it in a lovely old frame. Her body was there but her spirit was gone and Jim felt that as he passed the coffin, but still it was so good to be near her body one last time. He got his holy communion, turned to the right and he and Brendan caught each other's eye. So much feeling and understanding passed between them in that moment. They knew each other from work at Treacy's supermarket and Brendan had only just learnt on his mother's death bed that Jim is his real father. Heavy stuff in anybody's terms. They had been on the phone to each other several times since, with Jim not only giving lots of fatherly advice, but also getting Brendan's online bank details to transfer monies to pay for the whole funeral and whatever drinks and sandwiches they were having afterwards in the local gastropub for family, close friends and the few that go to all funerals just for the meal afterwards. There was an amazing warmth for both Jim and Brendan connecting up despite the total devastation of losing a lover and a mother. It was such a comfort to Brendan knowing that there was no problem paying for the funeral and the afters, especially as his siblings were in pandemic jail in Australia and weren't allowed home even for their mother's funeral. Livestream here, tears streaming in Australia. Their little brother having to be father, husband, family main man all in one, carrying the burden, lightened so much though having his real Dad around, though nobody knew.

Jim remained at the side aisle of the Cathedral as her coffin was shouldered towards the door and into the awaiting hearse, his chest up-tight, his whole body trying to stay strong and keep in the tears. The love of his life was being taken to her final place of rest. He slipped outside to the back of the crowd and waited to see the cortege drift away. Brendan looked around for him and they made one final eye-contact, knowing they'd be on the phone later. Jim thought it would be a step too far to go to the graveyard so there he said his last silent goodbye to his beloved Mary.

It was only about ten minutes walk back to his apartment, wandering through the streets near city centre, loads of people masked up out shopping with those gaunt soulless pandemic looks. For a moment Jim thought he would be quite happy to be taken out there and then, but changed when he thought of his two sons, one in particular who would need his support right now. He couldn't go back to his apartment, it was the middle of the day, well around one, and he'd just be sitting there remembering everything. As he was passing O'Shea's he thought he'd go in for some decent traditional city fayre and a pint to pass away an hour or so. The elderly waitress brought him the menu but he said "I'll just have the coddle and a pint please", real comfort food. He wasn't in the mood for looking at the menus and deciding on anything. He felt cold and drained having cried all the tears he had the night before, alone in his apartment. He was completely worn out. The waitress could see it in him, but no small talk could make any difference so she brought him over the newspaper. It's a comfortable olde worldy real city establishment with lots of antique furniture and the old red patterned carpet, just the comforting atmosphere he needed right now. It was good to get a bit of solid food into him, and a second pint. She brought him over tea and biscuits 'on the house'. All warmed up after this feed he felt positively sleepy and was beginning to nod off just sitting there at the table, the downside of pints during the day. Pure exhaustion knocked him out on the couch for a couple of hours when he got back, and then he woke again to the reality of being without his other half, wondering how can he ever get back up and going again?

To his surprise Brendan had made his way to near the apartment as Jim had mentioned roughly where it was, so two minutes after the phone call he had arrived. His last time there was as a six month suckling baby on his mother's breast. He brought back the photo for the album, and subconsciously needed to be with someone close, his new-found very own flesh and blood. It was great as a distraction but quite a shock for Jim to have Brendan there, in fact to have anybody there. He got a couple of cans out of the fridge. It was a bit shocking for Brendan also to realise that he was in another home of his mam's that he didn't ever know existed. Pictures of her everywhere, jewellery that he recognised up on the mantelpiece, not to mind loads of photos of himself! They had so much to talk about but it was just too soon and too raw to get into too much right now. They chatted about less important stuff, bits about work, who was at the funeral, the gathering afterwards, and not too much about Mary, they couldn't, they'd both well up. Jim already had a lot worked out, it was almost like he was planning his demise. He told Brendan that evening that he had decided to leave this apartment to him and he would be going to a solicitor the following week to make his will. That's a fairly big deal for a young fella these days in the city. They had another few cans before Brendan headed off home, and Jim went on to have a few whiskeys from a bottle that was usually there for medicinal purposes or the Christmas pudding, which Jim and Mary would do a special for just themselves. It was really out of character but poor Jim was in a bad sad place and he thought this would help.

Eyes were rolling the following morning when Jim arrived in around a quarter of an hour late for work. This was the first time in his long career that this had happened. He very obviously wasn't wearing a fresh shirt and tie, he was unshaven and really pretty shook looking. In a supermarket management setting this doesn't go unnoticed, but as it was a first offense his manager didn't say anything. Brendan was in early even though it was the morning after his mother's funeral. He didn't see any point in hanging around doing nothing on a weekday when it would only put more pressure on his colleagues at work. He was aware of Jims later arrival but couldn't say anything. Nobody must ever know their connection, it would be letting down the memory of Mary.

Jim's workmates in Treacy's supermarket could see he had gone all quiet, he was a different man. He'd be seen putting the vegetables out and his mind would be in a total other world, his heart wasn't in it anymore. When his son Graham from his marriage to Joanne had left boarding school and headed off to college in London he got rid of his car. There was no point in keeping it, traffic in the city had become chaotic, no more school runs at the weekend, no more matches, absolutely no need for a car in city centre. Since Mary got sick he'd slip in for a pint to his local last thing on his way home. Every evening now he couldn't face going back to the flat and sitting there for the night alone. After each shift now he'd get off the bus and slip into the pub for a few, and sometimes for a few more. Some evenings Brendan would give him a ring but he was fairly busy as

Mary's mother was still alive, so basically he worked all day and looked after his gran all night, and sher he met Jim at work anyway. Once a week or two Graham would ring. He was now a successful stockbroker in London, he didn't get good enough exam results to do law. He hardly ever came home and when he did they'd usually meet up in town for lunch. Last time he missed his call and couldn't get him on the mobile so he rang the landline. Joanne's partner Bryan answered the phone which was like a red rag to a bull. After about twenty eight years you'd think it would be ok but not to a man who's world had fallen apart who was going from the flat to work to the pub to the flat, with a little run into the late night shop for a sandwich, or the chipper, depending on the mood.

Jim was fairly 'well on' one night after having a few extra, and just coming along the path home came across this new girl standing there looking very sexy in her short tight skirt and very low cut top. "Hey handsome" she said with a wink "you looking for a bit of fun?" For some reason it didn't dawn on him that she was on the game, it was the wrong side of town for that. "Ah how'ya" says Jim "I'm just headin' home." "I will walk with you" she said. She was definitely foreign. "What's your name handsome?" "Jim, its Jim and yourself? "Well what would you like it to be?" Strange answer he thought, he was feeling fairly sozzled and braindead at this stage. He murmured "Mary" quietly "That's my name the young sexy beaut replied. "Jaysus that's amazin', I knew a girl called Mary" he said in a melancholy way. A few passers-by had big grins on their faces. "Oh its cold, isn't it" she said in a real cockney accent. "Jaysus its freezin', you'd want to wear warmer clothes around here at night." She was kinda rubbing up against him, touching him, grabbing his arm a little "you're a nice man" she said "do you live on your own?" "Yea" he said "I do now". There was no point in saying any more and she wasn't going to ask. One of their tricks is to always keep the conversation upbeat. "Ooh it's ever so cold" she said as she saw him beginning to slow down, obviously near his home. "Well here I am, this is my gaff up here. It was nice to meet you Mary." "I actually really need a pee, is there any chance...." "Ah yea, of course, c'mon up, that's no problem." A little bit of female company was warming the cockles of his drunken heart. "Oh wow Jim, nice place you go' 'ere." "Ah sher its ok you know" he said "the bathroom is over there." She came out with even less on than when she went in and at this stage she was definitely catching his eye, "Would you like a drop of something?" Jim asked. "You go' gin?" she replied. "Yea I think there's some there alright." Jim had nearly everything after his cocktail evenings with the real Mary. So he fixed her a drink and got himself a Jameson. "Are you not going out or something, all dressed up like that?" says Jim naively. "This is my first night 'on the stree', I'm new here I haven't done this before", and with that it hit Jim with a bang "Ah Jaysus you're, what would they say, 'working', oh god I'm sorry, I didn't want to invite you up for that." Trick number two came out of her sleeve "Oh no, I really needed a pee. I'm so afraid, afraid of who I'd meet, I'm terrified, and if I don't go back with at least a hundred and fifty I'm in trouble, my boss will kill me. I suppose I better go back out there." "Oh Jaysus that's awful. Sher I'll give you that and you can take the night off, listen

I'll get it there for you now in case I forget." A fake relief came over her face as she saw exactly which cupboard he went to for the cash. He seemed to take a wad out and put a lot back. "There you are, sher relax there and we'll have a coupe of drinks." She knew she had hit a jackpot. "We can always 'ave a little cuddle if you like Jim, and a bit more if you prefer" she said as she put the cash into her little bag. "Ah no, thanks anyway" he said half reluctantly "it's just lovely to have a little company, you know. I lost me missus a couple of months ago, well she wasn't me missus but you know, she was as good as." A perfect lead into trick number three ....

'About Jim'.....coming soon

Milton Keynes UK
Ingram Content Group UK Ltd.
UKHW030019180324
439604UK00001B/255